Wither

A BEAUTY AND THE BEAST INSPIRED MM NOVELLA

ASHLYN DREWEK

FOX HOLLOW BOOKS

Cover design by Artscandare Book Cover Design

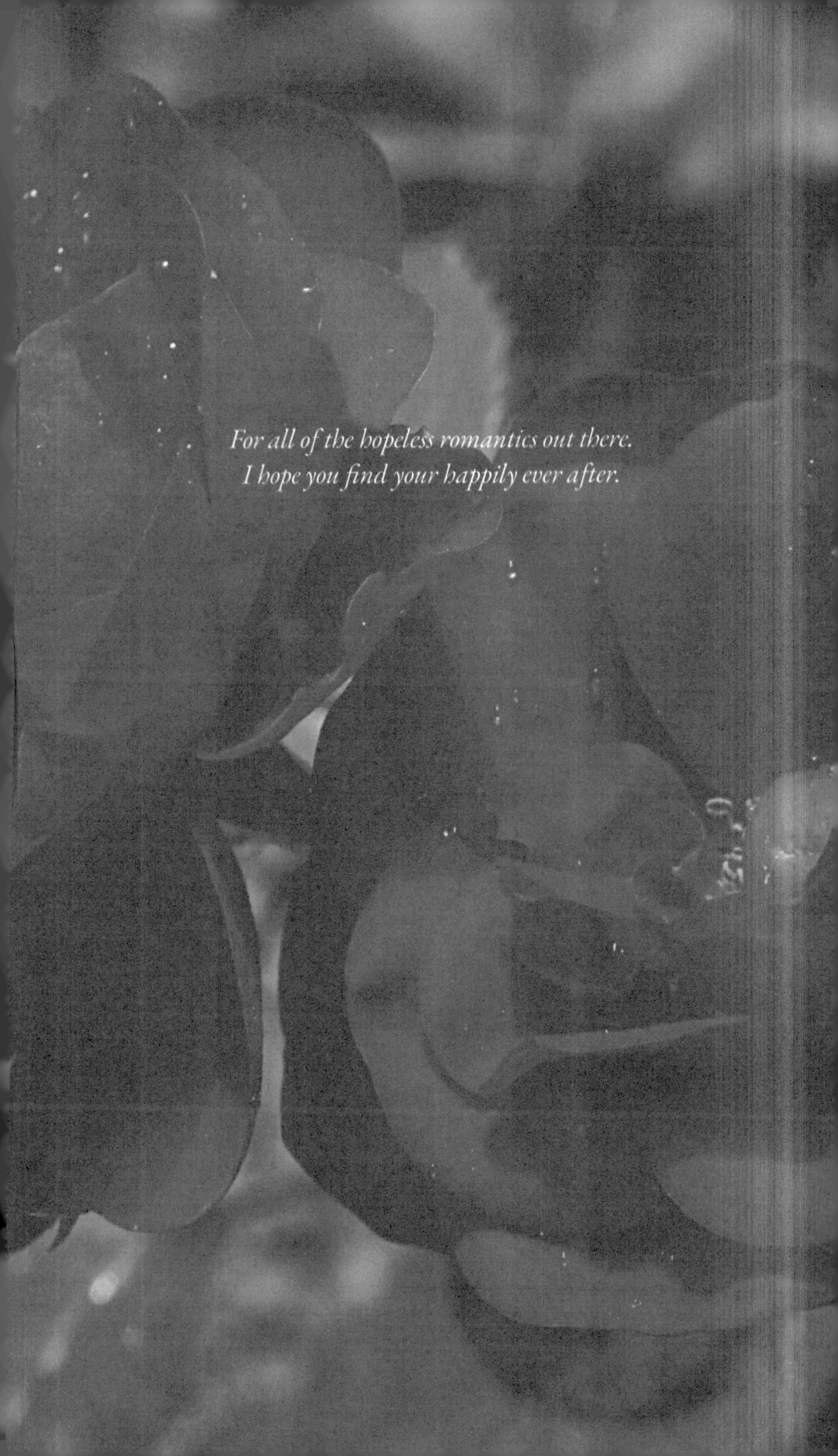

For all of the hopeless romantics out there.
I hope you find your happily ever after.

A warning to the reader

This book includes references to and depictions of sexual harassment; domestic abuse and violence; near-death accidents and disfigurement; and parental death. It is intended for a mature audience and reader discretion is advised.

Chapter One

ZANE

They say discretion is the better part of valor. Hiding in the children's section of the library, however, I wasn't so sure it was anything more than an attempt at dressing up cowardice into something more noble.

Clutching a stack of board books to my chest like they would provide an actual defense against the woman stalking me, I peeked out again through the shelving to see where she was.

It was absolutely ridiculous. I knew that. I might not have looked like it, but I was a grown man and I was literally hiding amongst children from a woman half my size. But size wasn't a detriment to Oksana. Nothing was, not even the word "No."

Prowling through the aisles like a jungle cat, her sharp eyes swept to and fro, taking note of every face she encountered. With a derisive sniff, she discarded their entire existence and carried on. Unfortunately for me and everyone else in the library, she wouldn't leave until she found the person she was hunting for.

"Do you have any books about dragons?" a tiny voice asked behind me.

I nearly jumped out of my skin and whirled around, taking in the pint-sized boy with a shock of red hair. "Dragons? Wh—what kind of dragons?"

"I don't know," he replied with a shrug, reassessing me with a bored expression. "That's why I asked you."

"Right." Oh my God, Zane! Get it together! "This way."

Offloading the armful of books onto the shelf, I made a note to come back for them later and led him over to the display of medieval fantasy books.

"Yeah!" As soon as he spied the books, he darted ahead of me, grabbing the one with a giant black dragon on the cover. He didn't waste any time flipping through it, chattering away to no one in particular about his thoughts on each and every picture or odd chapter title.

I couldn't help but smile, watching him with a sense of pride. Being a librarian wasn't the most exciting job in the world, but it was moments like that—where you watch a kid get *so* engrossed with a book they forget the outside world exists—that made the paltry salary and dust allergies worth it.

After the kid wandered away with his book, I lingered in the children's section a while longer, straightening the discarded books and tossing stray building blocks back into their bin.

"There you are."

I froze in place, eyes wide. The hair on the back of my neck stood on end like a mouse that had been caught. Pivoting slowly, I forced a polite smile to my face. "Oksana. Nice to see you." I cleared my throat, reinforcing the smile. "Again."

"I was beginning to think you changed your schedule on me again," she said with a faux pout, sauntering forward and sliding her fingertips up and down the strap on her gym bag, as if it was an enticement of some sort. I'm sure there were plenty of men who were dying to have her rake those blood-red claws across their skin, but I was *not* one of them.

"Esther's the one who makes the schedule, not me," I said, hoping my excuse sounded good. At the very least, I managed to seem equally disappointed. I mean, it wasn't a lie. Esther *did* make the schedule. But she happily changed my hours to whatever I needed, like pushing back my start time to avoid Oksana's yoga class in the studio next door.

My elderly boss also accommodated any last-minute requests for random days off whenever I saw Oksana loitering outside my apartment building. She even went so far as to *strongly* recommend I call the police one night when she spied Oksana leaning against my car in the parking lot. My would-be girlfriend was out there for over two hours, well past when the library closed, while Esther and I hid inside pretending to be busy.

As well-meaning as it was, I politely declined Esther's suggestion to involve the police. I mean, come on! A man calling the cops on a woman? For what? Excessive flirting? Not knowing how to respect someone's personal space? As annoying and somewhat dehumanizing as it was, I would have been laughed out of this town. There were people with far worse problems in the world than an exasperated gay man being pursued by a woman who couldn't take "No" for an answer.

"I wish that old hag would stop messing with you," Oksana said, brushing a wrinkle out of my shirt and smoothing the dark blue fabric over my chest like she was stroking a dog.

"She's not a hag. And she's not messing with me." A frown pulled at the corners of my mouth, for her rude remark and the fact I was two seconds away from flinging her hand off of me. Normally, I wasn't a touch-averse person, but she made my skin crawl. Each interaction seemed to leave her emboldened. The touches, in particular, were coming more and more frequently no matter what I said or how much distance I tried to put between us. One of these days, I was afraid she was going to maul me, and *then* what the hell was I supposed to do?

Thankfully, Oksana retracted her hand so she could toss her long, black hair over her shoulder. Batting her lashes, she smiled sweetly. “Have you had lunch yet? I’d love to go check out the bistro down the street.”

“I can’t. I’m the only one here today.” As if to prove my point, I sidestepped her and headed toward the circulation desk.

“Oh, perfect! I’ll bring it to you and we can have a picnic.”

“There’s no eating allowed in the library.”

Oksana pouted again, linking her arm through mine and walking with me for three measly steps, somehow managing to smash herself against me in the process. “Zane, you’re going to have to stop playing hard to get.”

“I’m not playing hard to get, Oksana. I’m gay. Remember?” I gently disentangled myself from her and rounded the desk for some more distance, even though I doubted a little swinging door was much of an obstacle. If we were alone, she’d probably go straight over it and pin me to the desk like a cougar before tearing me apart.

“That’s what all the pretty boys say,” she replied with a wave of her hand.

Sighing, I closed my eyes. Over the course of being acquainted with one another, I’d told her—repeatedly—I was gay. I didn’t know why she didn’t believe me, nor did I know what I was going to have to do to prove it. Although, I was pretty sure I could make out with the first random guy that came through the door and she still wouldn’t believe me. If anything, it might make the problem worse.

“Oksana...” I opened my eyes and cocked my head. “I really have a lot of work to do.”

She glanced around the library and the handful of patrons

scattered throughout. Arching a dark brow at me, she smiled nonetheless and ran a finger down the front of my chest, poking me lightly in the stomach. “You can’t avoid a date forever.”

“You don’t want to date me. I promise. I’m not as inter esting as you seem to think I am.”

“Yeah, you’re right,” she said, perching on the edge of the desk. Leaning on one arm, which conveniently pushed her ample cleavage into view beneath her barely-there sports bra, she batted her long, dark lashes. “I don’t want to date you. We’re going to get married one day. I can feel it.” I started to protest, but she kept going, a wistful look in her eyes. “Just picture it. Us in one of those cute little houses in the historic district; you taking over as the head librarian here; me running my photography business. We can have lunch together every day and pick our kids up from school. Oh, Zane. They’d be so beautiful! With your bone structure and my coloring?”

“My bone structure?” I quirked a brow at her.

“Excuse me,” an elderly woman huffed behind Oksana. Mrs. Nesbitt, God bless her! “I need to return these.”

Oksana glanced over her shoulder at the woman and scoffed. Before I had to tell her to get off the desk, she slid off on her own accord and gave me a dazzling smile. “I’ll see you tomorrow, Zane.”

“Have a nice night,” I mumbled, already dreading the next shift. If Esther didn’t have an appointment tomorrow afternoon, I would have totally called in sick. But I was also running out of sick time. Besides, I couldn’t hide from Oksana forever. Could I? I wondered if I could apply for some sort of short-term disability. Except, I needed my full paychecks, meager as they were, so it looked like the disability scheme was out.

As soon as Oksana walked away, Mrs. Nesbitt stepped forward and thunked a stack of random books on the desk.

"Have you thought about getting a restraining order? My nephew is a police officer. He could help you. Or maybe look for a different job? In a different town? I know Esther would be sad to lose you. We all would. But you can't even do your job without that little tart all over you. It's no way to live. You deserve more, Zane. At least say you'll think about it."

I pretended not to hear her and flipped through the books, scanning them into the system for the return. Except, none of them had a recent due date. "Some of these haven't been touched in over a year. Are you sure you checked them out at this library?"

Furrowing my brow, I looked up for the answer and gasped like an idiot. Mrs. Nesbitt was gone. There was absolutely no trace of her in the lobby and I knew for a fact she hadn't walked out. The front door was right next to the circulation desk and no one had gone out, or come in, since Oksana's departure.

"So weird..." I shook my head and moved the stack of books to the cart to be shelved later.

Underneath the last book was a section of the newspaper, folded up with a giant circle scribbled around one of the ads.

Curiosity more than anything prompted me to pick it up and see what Mrs. Nesbitt had marked with such enthusiasm.

It was a job posting. Subtle, ma'am. Very subtle.

More specifically, it stated **PERSONAL ASSISTANT.**

Personal assistant to an author needed for a six-month contract. Responsibilities include research, typing, editing, attending meetings, and personal errands. A nondisclosure agreement is required. Room/board provided along with weekly salary. Email: markabner@abnerandsons.com

A weekly salary was obviously nice, but throw in room and board? I could actually save up some money *and* learn from a successful author. Maybe one day it would help me publish a book of my own, but more importantly, it meant I would finally have enough money to take care of my dad. I could move him to a new facility, where they could really work on his rehabilitation. Then maybe one day he could come home again...

While the ad didn't say which author the job was for, there were only a handful of probable candidates in this part of the country with the kind of prestige that would necessitate an NDA. Most of them were based in or around Chicago, according to their bios, which meant it was highly unlikely for them to be looking for an assistant this far in the western suburbs. Still, depending on who the author was, it could be the opportunity of a lifetime. Either way, it was a guaranteed break from Oksana.

I emailed them immediately.

Chapter Two

GERULF

"You're late," I snapped as soon as the door to my office swung open. I didn't bother turning around to face the tall, skinny man ambling in. I could see him just fine in the reflection of the window.

"I was handling another matter," Mark Abner replied. He hesitated for a moment, glancing between me and the chair in front of my desk, as if trying to decide how rude it would be to sit while I stood.

"What other matter?"

"Your agent called."

"You mean my agent or my backstabbing bitch of an ex-fiancée?" I shot back, not even giving him time to answer. "She already ruined my life. What could she possibly want now?"

Mark ignored the question. "They've already extended your contract by six months, despite not having a rough draft. I don't know how much longer I can hold them off. It's already been over two years. You have to give them *something*."

"What do you want me to do? The words won't come! And having her breathing down my neck after she knows goddamn well what I've been through isn't going to help!" I clenched my fist against the windowsill, doing everything in my power not to punch through the glass. Although at this point, what were a few more scars to add to the collection? The only thing really holding me back was the cost to replace the custom window. "*She's* the reason I'm in this situation in the first place! Did you remind her of that?"

"I know. Ok? That's why I've taken the liberty of hiring you a personal assistant. *Again.*"

"You what?!" I whirled away from the window that time, staring him down with one furious eye as I closed the distance in long strides. "What did I tell you the last time?! I don't *want* a personal assistant! Or an intern or whatever the fuck you want to call it!"

"He's a writer. He can help you—" He flinched with my rapid approach, but remained where he was, clearing his throat before trying again. "Don't fight this, Gerulf. You need help. *Real* help. Help no one else around here has been able to give you. You've fired the last six assistants without even meeting them. Just *try* to give this one a chance!"

"I don't 'need' anything, least of all some stranger poking around in my life! After everything I've done to avoid the media, I can't believe you would throw all that away without even talking to me! How do you know he's not some reporter in disguise? Someone who's going to snap a few pictures of the hideous beast and sell them to the highest bidder? For all you know, Faye fucking sent him here to spy on me!"

Mark frowned. "He's not a spy, I assure you. And he's already signed a Non-Disclosure, so the media won't be a problem. Plus he idolizes you. He'll do whatever you say. He'd probably be happy taking out your trash."

"Wonderful. Just what I 'need,'" I snarled, stalking away from my traitorous lawyer and back to the window, inadvertently catching a glimpse of myself in the glass before I turned away in disgust. "Some sycophant trying to wheedle their way into my good graces so I'll read their fucking book or give them a favorable review. As if I don't have enough to deal with already. Now you expect me to graciously accept the help I never asked for to finish a book I don't want to fucking write!"

"Accept the help, don't accept the help. It doesn't really matter what you say. It's a done deal and he's staying."

"The hell it is!" I whirled back around, my blood pressure spiking once more. "Contracts are broken every goddamn day."

"Then go tell him yourself. He's in the library waiting for you." Mark shrugged and crossed his arms over his chest. "Go ahead."

Rage flooded every cell in my body. Goddamn him! He was calling my bluff, thinking I'd be too scared to show my face to someone outside these walls. Well, the joke was on him because today I was pissed off enough to do it.

Storming away from the window, I glared at Mark as I cut across my office, vowing silently to eviscerate him on the page for this little stunt. The heavy door banged against the wall when I yanked it open, echoing throughout the house and announcing to everyone I was on the warpath.

I heard Mark scurrying behind me as my steps thundered down the hallway to the library. Throwing the double doors open, I marched inside and scanned the enormous room for any sign of this new interloper.

He wasn't hard to spot.

The first thing I saw was a mass of curly brown hair skimming narrow shoulders. Warm brown eyes landed on mine, followed by a smile that lit up his whole face—a smile that didn't falter even when I stopped abruptly, my jaw slack. For a split second, I didn't know if he was a *he* at all. With his high cheekbones, plush lips, and perfect, unblemished skin, he was nothing if not beautiful.

I hated him.

I hated everything about him.

On the flip side, if *he* was horrified by *my* appearance, he didn't let on. I didn't even catch a glimmer of disgust. He wasn't a writer then. He was an actor. A gifted actor, I would begrudgingly admit, with a face that was too pretty to belong to a man.

"Hi! I'm Zane, Zane Beaumont." He rushed forward the rest of the way, sticking his hand out like an eager Boy Scout. "It's such an honor to meet you. I'm a massive fan of your work. And I just wanted to thank you for the opportunity to—"

"Shut the fuck up and get out of my house."

He blinked, his hand dropping slowly. Finally, his smile started to fade. "Excuse me?"

"Did I stutter? Get out!"

Maybe he was deaf. Or dumb. There had to be some sort of explanation as to why he just stood there, mouth agape like a damn guppy.

"Sir, the tea is ready in the solarium," Gilroy said from the doorway, as pleasant as could be. As if he didn't notice I wasn't seconds from throwing this intruder out the window and onto the front lawn, glass repairs be damned.

"I don't want any fucking tea!" I snapped at my butler, as much for the interruption as for letting Mark bring someone into the house without my permission. The vein in my forehead spasmed, adding to the terrible thumping building inside my skull. One more minute of this nonsense and I'd be bedridden for the next twenty-four hours. Logically, I knew Zane Beaumont wasn't worth a migraine, but my anger wasn't listening to logic at the moment.

"I was speaking to Mr. Beaumont," Gilroy replied loftily.

Zane glanced between the butler and me, clearly trying to decide whom he should listen to. The fact he even questioned who the real master of the house was had me seeing red.

Fury and humiliation warred inside me. Before I came completely unhinged and popped a blood vessel, I spun on the ball of my foot and headed for the door. Something solid slammed into my left side, sending sparks of pain radiating throughout my broken body. I stumbled to my right but I had to swing my head fully toward the left, like some lumbering brute, to see what the hell I ran into.

Gilroy was in the midst of regaining his own footing. He straightened and smoothed down his tie, offering me a small nod. At least he had the forethought not to try and muster up some lame excuse or give any verbal acknowledgment whatsoever of our collision. It was bad enough it happened in the first place, especially in front of company.

It didn't matter that my entire left side was a giant blindspot, I should have apologized to him since I was unquestionably the one at fault. Instead, I swept through the doorway, rubbing my crippled shoulder and cursing everything about this miserable day and the depressing farce that was my life.

Chapter Three

ZANE

Wow. They say you should never meet your heroes and I guess they were right. Gerulf Prince was *nothing* like I imagined.

When I pulled up to the gates of the massive house in the middle of nowhere, I thought my GPS was obviously off. But whoever answered the speaker box told me they were expecting me and buzzed me through.

The house was straight out of a fairytale—a large, castle-like structure composed of red brick and half-timber framing. It had a turret. A *turret*! And so many chimneys sticking up out of the roofline I lost count. It looked like it belonged on a rolling hillside in France, not in the middle of Illinois cornfields.

It felt weird parking my car next to a fountain in the circular drive, but I didn't know where else I was supposed to put it. It's not like I saw a garage somewhere. So I crossed my fingers and hoped for the best.

A severe-looking man in a black suit answered the door and led me through the house in silence. Literal suits of armor lined one hallway and some of the ceilings were painted with cherubs and chivalric scenes from the Renaissance. The house obviously wasn't *that* old, but the way it was designed and decorated definitely made you forget you were living in the twenty-first century.

My silent tour guide led me to the library and introduced me to another man in a suit. "Mr. Abner, Mr. Beaumont for you."

"Thank you, Gilroy," Mr. Abner said with a smile, shaking my hand. "Thank you for making the drive on such short notice. Please, sit."

I forced myself to stop staring at the floor-to-ceiling walls of books and focus on my interviewer. "Thank you for the opportunity."

"Yes, well, you might not be thanking me by the end of it," he said with a chuckle. "If you wouldn't mind signing this first, then we can begin." He slid a piece of paper across the coffee table and set a heavy pen on the page.

"What is this?" I asked, scanning the long legal explanations beneath a title that clearly said *Non-Disclosure Agreement*.

"An NDA. I'm afraid it's necessary for all of the staff. Are you a reader, Mr. Beaumont? Or a writer, perchance?"

"Zane," I replied, scribbling my name at the bottom and handing him the agreement and his pen. "And yes, to both. I graduated with my master's degree in library science last May, but I haven't published anything of my own yet. Just a couple short stories in some anthologies. Nothing big."

"Wonderful. Have you heard of Gerulf Prince?"

"Have I—yeah! I mean, yes! I've heard of him. He's..." I couldn't even find the words since I was still trying to pick my jaw up off the floor. I was in Gerulf Prince's house. Gerulf fucking Prince! He wasn't even on my list of potential authors because he's *Gerulf Prince*, one of the most prolific writers of our time.

To say he was a literary genius was something of an understatement. Worldwide recognition, shelves full of awards, and millions in royalties. There wasn't any genre he couldn't tackle. That's partly how he made his name—blending tropes and sub-genres, churning out twisty plots and characters with such complexity you'd swear they were flesh-and-blood people. The world was eagerly awaiting his next release, a historical thriller set in late nineteenth-century Chicago. So far, no one knew anything about it except the buzz generated by the press about why it was taking so long. It was bound to be another award winner, they said.

Then again, I imagined he'd had a hard time since his car accident. Two years ago, the literary world was devastated to learn he nearly died while vacationing in Switzerland over the holidays. Reports said he'd been hospitalized for months.

After that, any information about him sort of dwindled to nothing until last year, when his name was splashed all over the headlines again thanks to someone leaking the title of his work in progress, something nebulously called *Loss of Twilight.* The publishing house and his literary agency blamed each other, meanwhile, his fans went rabid. Even though there wasn't any sort of synopsis or a cover design to go with the title, the book nerds spent months theorizing what it could possibly be about, but no one knew definitively. If things went well with this interview, I'd be at the center of all the action. The bookworm inside rejoiced.

"I'm sure you know about Gerulf's accident," Mr. Abner said, continuing after I nodded. "Some of the rumors were, unfortunately, true. He was badly injured and that has led to a delay in writing. He's under contract and if he doesn't give them something, he's facing dire legal consequences. Now, money he can handle, as you can see," he said, gesturing around the massive library. "But with a legal battle comes publicity and Gerulf is adamant no one sees what has happened to him. It's a sore subject, to say the least."

"What happened to him?" I asked quietly.

"Superficially, he's scarred very badly on the left side of his body. When the car crashed, his side took the brunt of the impact. He was impaled on part of the door, causing a variety of nerve and muscle damage. He also lost the use of his left eye and learning to adjust to monocular vision has not been easy for him. Which is where you, potentially, come in.

"He needs someone who can do the writing for him, take his dictation and make it into a story. He can still use a pen but depending on the day, he doesn't have the dexterity for typing, so this would relieve some of the pressure to finish the book. He also can't read for long periods of time anymore without getting debilitating migraines. Likewise, you'd also have to proofread what he's already done before it's sent to the editor.

"Other jobs might include running errands for him, taking him to appointments, reading to him, researching something for the story. Whatever he needs to help make his life easier so he can get this damn book finished by the middle of January."

I nodded. Honestly, I'd pick up Gerulf's dry cleaning if he wanted me to and do it with a smile. Anything to help one of my favorite authors accomplish his next project. "Yeah. Absolutely. I understand. I'm happy to do whatever he needs."

Mr. Abner went over a few other details and asked about my background, the usual back-and-forth interview questions. At the end of it, he smiled and laced his fingers together in his lap. "One final question, Zane."

"Of course."

"How do you handle conflict?"

For some reason, I immediately thought of Oksana. I hedged, trying to decide how best to answer him. Finally, I went with the truth instead of trying to sound suave. "I don't.

I try to find a way to avoid it or diffuse the situation. Cooler heads prevail, right?"

His smile broadened. "Excellent. I'd like to officially offer you the position." He withdrew another contract and slid it across the table. "The terms of your employment, along with the salary and a list of other benefits."

"Really?" I blinked and gave myself a mental slap for sounding like a complete moron. I mean, it had been a good interview, but normally you had to wait days or weeks to hear back from a company. Although in this case, they were clearly making an exception since Gerulf had a nonnegotiable deadline to meet.

"Yes, really. Time is of the essence. I need you to start right away. As in, tonight, if you're able."

"Yes, of course. I mean, thank you! I don't know what to say." A split second after I said it, I realized I should have probably looked at the contract before agreeing to anything.

"I hope you say you'll take it."

Flipping through the pages, my eyes nearly bugged out of my head at the salary listed. There were more zeros on that number than I'd ever had on a paycheck in my life. If I saw this thing through, I'd have enough money to help my dad *and* some left over for a nest egg. Only an idiot would turn it down.

As soon as I signed the contract, Mr. Abner excused himself to go find Gerulf. He instructed me to wait in the library and said he'd just be a minute. I heard him mutter, "Hopefully," under his breath as he hurried away.

I'd been confused by that last part, but after meeting Gerulf Prince in the flesh, I understood what his lawyer had been trying to tell me without explicitly telling me. I couldn't even begin to fathom what Gerulf had been through, but the jury was still out on whether or not that entitled him to act like a dick to a perfect stranger.

After Gerulf stormed out of the library, I was left quaking in my shoes, stunned by both the abrupt dismissal and, well, *him*.

I'd be lying if I said I didn't notice what he looked like. How could you *not* notice? The man pictured on the back of his books was striking—dark hair, tan skin, a face chiseled to perfection, and pale eyes that somehow pierced your soul from a simple photograph.

But now I knew why no one had seen in him in so long.

The right side of his face still belonged on a magazine; the left, however, was more suited to a horror novel. A nasty, jagged red scar ran vertically down the left side of his face, splitting his dark brow and slashing across his left eye, leaving it an unsettling white color. There were other deep scars on his left cheek, disappearing into his hairline and down into the collar of his black button-up shirt. Just below his jaw, a patch of marbled skin peeked out of his shirt collar, leftover evidence of some sort of burn. Despite the summer heat, he'd been wearing long sleeves and pants, so I didn't know what the rest of him looked like, but I'm sure it wasn't good.

Beyond the psychological toll associated with such disfigurement, I'm sure it was physically painful too. And who knew how the loss of his eye really impacted him on a day-to-day basis, aside from the migraines and the inability to work independently. I mean, I imagined it was pretty bad if he had to resort to hiring a PA to finish his novel. Then again, maybe *he* didn't plan on hiring anyone since he was extraordinarily pissed when he came into the room, which meant it was all Abner's doing. I could see both sides of the situation, his and his lawyer's, but I had no idea where that left me.

"If you'll follow me, please," Gilroy said, reminding me I was standing there like a dope.

My heart sank. Each step I took toward the door felt like

slogging through quicksand. I didn't want to go, but I wasn't going to stay when I clearly wasn't wanted either.

Instead of leading me to the front door, Gilroy took me to another part of the house I hadn't seen on the way in.

"Where are we going?" I asked, staring at the paintings lining the hallways. A mix of landscapes and portraits, they added to the air of old sophistication the house exuded, almost like it was caught in a time capsule.

"The solarium."

"But Mr. Prince wanted me to leave."

"If you're going to work for Mr. Prince, you'll have to learn to navigate between what he says he wants and what he actually needs. They are not always the same thing."

"Isn't that, like, insubordinate?"

"Perhaps. But in this house, the ends justify the means."

Um... ok. Pretty sure I'd never read *that* in any HR handbook. "Why did Mr. Abner hire me?"

"You would have to ask Mr. Abner," Gilroy replied with a bored tone.

"I'm just saying, it seemed like a bit of a... shock to Mr. Prince. It didn't seem like he knew what was going on when he came in the room."

"Mr. Prince is not used to having visitors anymore or interacting with new people face-to-face. Give him time and he will come around to you. Hopefully."

Gilroy opened the door to an all-glass room filled with a variety of potted plants and greenery. A fountain built into the brick wall of the house gurgled quietly. Dozens of red rose bushes perfumed the air. Some climbed up white trellises while others spilled out of concrete planters. A black wrought iron table and chairs sat in the center of the room, a tea cart positioned next to them.

"Enjoy your tea, sir."

"Uh, thanks." I gave him a fleeting smile and walked through the door he was holding.

Alone again, I looked around the solarium as I made my way to the table. Easing into the chair, I helped myself to a cucumber sandwich and took a tentative bite.

The fact that two of Gerulf's employees used the word "hopefully" when discussing the outcome of this contract didn't exactly give me warm fuzzies.

I had no idea what I was going to do now. Gilroy heard the order for me to leave, yet he brought me here. Would I stay for the six months anyway? Knowing Gerulf didn't want me here? Or would I collect my salary and go? I'd signed a contract with the lawyer and *I* certainly wasn't the one who broke it.

As tempting as it was to walk away with a good chunk of money for doing absolutely nothing, the notion didn't sit well with me. It didn't matter that Gerulf had millions and I had none. Taking his money without actually earning it was tantamount to stealing, no matter how good of a reason I had.

Two tea sandwiches and a cranberry-orange scone later and I still didn't have an answer for myself.

The door opened again. I jumped to my feet, fully expecting to see Gerulf barging through it. To my relief, the elderly woman who wandered in was anything but terrifying.

"How's it going, love?" she asked with a smile, walking right past me and touching her fingers to the teapot. "Would you like me to bring more?"

"No, I'm fine. Thank you."

"Sit, sit." She flapped a hand at me until I followed her instruction.

"I'm Zane," I offered lamely, even though I didn't know if it mattered at this point.

"Mrs. Potter, the housekeeper. You let me know if you need anything at all during your stay and I'll get it sorted."

"Stay? But Mr. Prince—"

"Yes, I heard. The whole house heard. Never mind him, dear. He's always had a dreadful temper and I'm afraid it's only gotten worse since the accident. You'll just have to learn to ignore it. These days, it's the pain speaking, not him. It helps to remember that."

"So you think I should stay?"

"Of course I do. He needs the help but he would rather die than admit it to anyone."

"I know. Mr. Abner said his literary agent is threatening to sue him if he doesn't produce a rough draft in the next six months."

She laughed and waved me off. "Oh, I'm not talking about that wretched woman. I was talking about Gerulf's craft. He lost his muse, you see. Ever since the accident, maybe even before... We've all tried to help him get it back, but I think it's going to take another writer to reach him."

"Oh, I'm a librarian. I'm not an author."

"I didn't say another author. I said a writer. And yes, there *is* a difference." She smiled and patted my shoulder, heading for the door again. "Use the bell pull when you're finished. Gilroy will take you to your room."

"But I don't have any stuff with me. I need to go home and pack a bag or something." If I even decided to stay. The jury was still out on that verdict, too.

"Well, make sure you come back in time for dinner. Chef's got a pot roast on that you don't want to miss."

"Oh, but I still don't—"

"Just run home and get some of your clothes. We have everything else you need right here." She closed the door behind her, literally shutting the door on our conversation—if you could call it that.

I watched her leave, brows furrowed, trying to make sense of everything she'd said. How did she know I wanted to be an author, anyway? Was she eavesdropping on the interview? For some reason, I wouldn't have been surprised in a place like this. And what did she mean they had everything I needed? That was weird, considering Gerulf didn't seem like the type to host long-term guests, which Gilroy more or less said. Or maybe she meant they'd send someone to the store to pick up some stuff.

Strange as it was, I guess I had my answer.

At the very least, I had a feeling the next six months were going to be interesting.

Chapter Four

GERULF

The pain started before I even opened my eyes, an excruciating thumping on the left side of my head. It was probably from all the shouting. Even though I knew it would lead to this yesterday, in the midst of my furor I did it anyway. All because no matter what I said, my staff seemed to think they knew better than I did. I felt like a child again—yelling at the top of my lungs for my parents' attention, only to be continuously ignored until the day my imagined orphanhood became a reality.

Since I could only deal with one tragedy at a time, I shoved Mom and Dad to the back burner and focused on the more pressing issue, namely the pain chipping away at what remained of my brittle sanity. Rolling over, I snagged one of the pill bottles off the side table and unscrewed it. I tossed a couple of pills back and swallowed them down with a glass of water, waiting impatiently for them to kick in.

I laid there for at least another half hour, listening to the house come alive around me as the staff went about their tasks. From the faint smell of coffee and bacon floating through the air, I knew breakfast was about ready. As much as I wanted to stay in bed and ignore the world, I had to get up. Moving was crucial to my never-ending recovery. Agonizing, but crucial. God knew I couldn't afford to lose any more muscle mass or mobility.

Heaving myself out of bed, I stumbled into the bathroom, once again confronting the giant blank space above the marble sink. The dark blue wallpaper had faded over the years, except for the patch of perfectly preserved color where the mirror used to hang. One of these days I was going to have to make a decision about what to do with it—either re-wallpaper the whole bathroom or hang something else up, like a painting.

Pain started creeping around the front of my skull again, so I quit thinking about the fucking wallpaper and the reason I had to concern myself with interior design shit in the first place.

I didn't need a mirror to be reminded of how grotesque I was. I could feel it, deep in my bones where they'd broken and healed and in the tight, unforgiving scar tissue all over my body. Perhaps if I'd been ugly before the accident, the end result wouldn't bother me so much. Vain as it was, I knew I'd been handsome. I prided myself on it. Everyone knew it didn't matter how brilliant you were—unless your brain came wrapped in a pretty package, no one cared. The world wasn't nice to unattractive people and there were plenty of studies to prove it.

My face had opened dozens of doors to me; got me meetings with top literary agents and publishers, landed me coveted TV and magazine interviews, and, of course, made me a darling in the society pages. And I loved it. I loved the attention. Because for the first time in my life I was getting it—people *noticed* me.

They still noticed me now, but not in the way I ever wanted. That car crash had ruined everything. Absolutely everything. In the blink of an eye, I lost my career, my fiancée, my very identity.

Technically, I was still an author, even if it had been years since I published anything.

Technically, my fiancée was still alive, except she was waltzing around as my *ex*-fiancée and bitch of an agent.

And, yeah, somehow I still had a pulse, no matter how often I wished I'd died that day. People told me to be grateful I was alive, but what good was that when children literally cried when they saw me? Now those same people didn't even pick up the phone when I called. They couldn't bear to have their picture-perfect lives tainted by something as hideous as me, a constant reminder that it didn't matter how rich or stunning you were, you could lose it all in a heartbeat.

Other than the requisite doctors' appointments, I didn't leave the estate anymore. Shutting myself off from people was easier than enduring their horrified gasps and pitying looks. I interacted with a small circle of necessary employees as needed and that was it. That is until my oh-so-helpful lawyer took it upon himself to hire yet another person I didn't need nor want in my life. You'd think he would have gotten the hint after I fired the last six assistants he tried to force on me. At least that latest doe-eyed kid was back in Chicago or wherever they scrounged him up from, regaling his friends with tales of the monstrous freak he'd had the misfortune of meeting. Fucking Mark. It was seriously time to consider finding a new lawyer.

Once I was dressed, I made my way down to breakfast, navigating the stairs carefully and clutching the railing like an eighty-year-old man. I couldn't even remember how many times I'd tripped or actually fallen down them. Depth perception was a real bitch when you only had one eye to work with and the reaction time of a sloth. That was yet another thing taken from me prematurely—any semblance of dignity. Another tick in the "I'd rather be dead" column.

Heading into the dining room, I spied a mop of brown curls and came to an abrupt halt. Zane was seated at the far end of the table, right next to my place setting, enjoying breakfast from the looks of it. Defiant son of a bitch.

"What the fuck are you doing?" I asked, marching up to the man as he speared another piece of French toast on his plate.

"Having breakfast," he replied with a smile that was entirely too fucking chipper for a trespasser. "Good morning, by the way."

"I told you to get out! Do I have to call the police and have you thrown out?"

"Um, there's a note from your lawyer," Zane said, motioning with his fork toward my seat. "He said you might want to read it before you call the police."

Seething, I stomped to the end of the table and snatched the letter off my plate, ripping it open.

Gerulf,

He'll be paid his full salary plus a generous severance package if you terminate his contract before the six months is up. It will cost you a small fortune and probably bankrupt you completely. Yes, I know I'm an asshole and yes, I did it on purpose because you need help.

I'd advise you to make good use of your time with him. He's been the best candidate so far. Try to keep your temper. You definitely can't afford a lawsuit if you hit him, plus you know your mugshot would go viral.

Trust me. And don't take it out on the guy. He just wants to help.

—Mark

Crumpling up the letter, I threw it to the ground with

only a minimal growl. God-fucking-damn him! Goddamn *both* of them! Could this day get any fucking worse?!

Mrs. Potter swept in the door, carrying a fresh tray. "Good morning, sir."

"Is it?" I snapped.

"Chef's made all of your favorites this morning," she replied with a smile as bright as Zane's, like a couple of co-conspirators. Setting the tray down next to my place setting, she lifted the silver dome and began removing more plates—French toast, eggs, bacon cooked the way I liked, and fresh-squeezed orange juice to go along with the cup of black coffee.

Even though I desperately needed to eat before all the medication made me nauseated, I still didn't make any sort of move to drag my chair out from the table. "So I see. This wouldn't be some sort of attempt at placating me, would it?"

"Never, dear. Sit and eat before it gets cold."

"I think I'll take my breakfast in the solarium." I slid a glare in Zane's direction, noting he'd gone silent since Mrs. Potter arrived. His silverware had stopped moving and he sat there, as still as a statue, watching us like a tennis match with those solemn brown eyes of his.

"I'm afraid that's not possible," Mrs. Potter replied.

I glared at her, arching the brow above my good eye. "Why not?"

"The gardener is power washing the floors."

"Then the library."

"Oh, I'm afraid Lisette is dusting."

I folded my arms over my chest, exhaling a slow breath through my nose to try and keep my blood pressure from spiking through the roof again. "My office?"

"Itzel is cleaning the windows."

"Then send all of this to my room!"

"Of course, sir, but today is the day Gilroy changes out the—"

"Enough of your nonsense, woman! If I can't eat in peace in my own house, then I won't eat at all!" I sidestepped her and stormed out of the dining room as fast as I could. I really didn't have a destination in mind, all I knew was that I wanted to get away from the two of them and their curious stares, like they were both waiting for me to explode. Which... I nearly did.

Itzel opened the door to my office, took one look at me, and promptly slammed it shut again. It didn't matter since I bypassed it, *and* the library, and continued down the hall. I should have gone to the kitchen for a piece of fruit or something to put in my stomach, but I threw open the side door and escaped into the morning sunlight.

Closing my eyes against the harsh light, I followed the sound of gravel crunching beneath my shoes and headed for the gardens.

Did they think I was oblivious to what they were doing? That they could pull my strings like I was a goddamn brainless puppet? Somehow they'd all gotten it in their heads I needed help. I didn't. I didn't need anything, except to be left the hell alone. To not have everyone fawning over me and trying to do things for me like I was completely inept, or scheming behind my back like I was a fucking moron. It was both infantilizing *and* infuriating.

In case they all forgot, *I* was the one under contract to write the fucking book and I'd write it when *I* was damn good and ready. Faye and the rest of the vultures at the publishing house could rot in hell as far as I was concerned. I lost my eye and some motor function on my left side; I didn't have a goddamn lobotomy!

Veering off the main gravel path, I followed a smaller one to the rose garden. Their heady scent hung in the air, combined with freshly mown grass. I stopped and cradled a dark red bloom. Morning dew clung to the velvety petals, glinting in the sunlight. Try as I might to find some beauty in this pathetic world, I came up empty time and again, even in the presence of my mother's majestic garden.

They were heirloom roses, she told me. It meant they smelled better than modern rose bushes and were hardier, able to survive the inevitable winter. They were in full bloom, basking in the summer sunlight, and would remain that way through the fall. But soon enough, all of the petals would wither and fade, like everything else in life. I envied them. They'd live and die without ever being seen as anything but the most regal flower in the garden. No one could look at a rose and be horrified by its appearance. I, on the other hand, would never again know what it was like to be looked upon with admiration, only revulsion.

I sank onto a stone bench and considered the roses in front of me. *Loss of Twilight* needled the back of my mind, begging for inspiration, a sentence or two. *Anything*. But I had nothing. Whatever plot I'd formed once upon a time was gone, along with any sense of passion for the project. The pressure to write it, from industry professionals and the readers themselves, only added to my foul mood. They all wanted something I couldn't give them. I couldn't give them anything else, either, because of the fucking contract!

Stewing in my never-ending bitterness, it wasn't long before I heard someone else coming down the gravel walkway. I didn't bother turning my head. Hopefully, it was one of the gardeners, who would keep walking and leave me the hell alone. It was bad enough I'd already been chased out of my damn house by a Boy Scout and Mrs. Potter's painfully obvious, half-brained idea of setting up a playdate for me. The staff ate in the kitchen and if I was ultimately paying him to be here, then that made him fucking *staff*.

The footsteps changed direction. Instead of continuing on

their way, or turning back for the house, they headed straight for me.

"Go away," I snarled, still not bothering to turn around.

"I brought you some breakfast," a soft male voice said. Zane. As if the day couldn't get any worse.

"Apparently you missed the part where I said I'm not hungry."

"No, you said you weren't eating. That's not the same thing. And Mrs. Potter said you need to eat first thing in the morning." He kept walking, undeterred by the glower on my face and unaware of the danger he was putting himself in. I could strangle him in this garden and no one would know. I could snap his neck like a twig and turn him into fertilizer. Smash his forehead into the stone bench. I could do whatever I wanted and make him disappear in the blink of an eye; it's not like the staff would turn me in. I wrote about murderers for a living—I was quite literally capable of anything if I had a mind to. Whether or not my body was capable of carrying it out was another matter I preferred not to think about.

Zane set the items on my left, something metal and something like crinkled paper. After a split second, he snatched them up again and moved them to my right. A thermos and something wrapped in brown paper, reminiscent of a sandwich. "Sorry about that," he murmured, stepping back and shoving his hands in his jeans pockets.

"Sorry about what? Staying when your presence isn't welcome? Taking my money when I didn't offer it to you? Or is that a pathetic bid at expressing sympathy for me? Tell me, Zane"—I couldn't help but snort at his name, though I had absolutely no room to talk—"what are you so *sorry* for?"

"For putting your breakfast on the left side, where you can't—" He cut himself off by clearing his throat. "It won't happen again."

I got to my feet slowly, ignoring the queasy rumble in my

stomach, and took a step forward. We were eye-level with one another, but even with my physical disadvantage, I had a feeling I could still overpower him with relative ease. Tall and thin, he was like a reed, seconds away from breaking in half if a strong enough wind came along—or a writer with enough motivation.

Despite the invasion into his personal space, Zane held his ground, his pointy chin tipped up in defiance. His big brown eyes narrowed and his jaw clenched. It was like watching a puppy get mad at an older, bigger dog, desperate to prove itself as an equal.

"It won't happen again," I repeated, fixing him with a glare, "because you're not staying for another six minutes, let alone six months. Now get your shit and get out of my house."

"Respectfully, I was hired to do a job and I'm going to do it."

"Is that a fact?"

"That's a fact."

"You're pretty brave for a twelve-year-old."

He smirked. "You're not as scary as I'm sure you'd like to think you are."

My hand flashed out, seizing him by the throat. I hauled him forward, giving him an up close and personal view of the left side of my face. To my surprise, he didn't look at it. He yelped and clung to my wrist, but his wide-eyed gaze remained focused on my good eye.

"Am I scary now?" I asked between my teeth.

The muscles under my hand constricted with a swallow, but he shook his head. "No."

"Go ahead. Take a good look at the monster you're so desperate to work for. Get it out of your system. Sate the curiosity. Make sure you get every detail right to tell all your little friends."

"You're not a monster." His expression softened and his

reply came with such conviction I was tempted to believe him, but ultimately I knew better. People said all sorts of conciliatory things when confronted with the threat of physical harm. Why would he be any different?

I considered him for another moment, the way his breathing hitched and how warm his fingers were wrapped around my wrist. Not once in all the time he stood there did his dark gaze divert to the left side of my face. I could count on one hand the number of times I'd been met with *that* reaction instead of the customary gawping, gasping, or whispering. As much as I hated him and hated the idea of someone new and unknown in my house, his decency meant he wasn't the most miserable human being I'd ever encountered in thirty-seven years. I suppose that was saying something.

"If you want to be useful, go get my laptop," I said at last, shoving him away from me.

He stumbled backward, touching his throat instinctively. Swallowing, he gave a terse nod and disappeared the way he came.

As soon as he was safely out of earshot, I laughed at the absurdity of it all. This kid wouldn't last the week. And you'd better be damn sure that when *he* broke the contract, he wasn't getting a dime of my money.

Chapter Five

ZANE

Mrs. Potter said Gerulf had a "dreadful temper," but that little stunt back there seemed a couple of steps above "dreadful." More like murderous? Deranged? I mean, I knew he'd been through a lot, but Jesus! With how hard he grabbed my throat, I wouldn't have been surprised if he left bruises. Did Ábner include hazard pay in that contract? I made a mental note to reread it at some point, just to make sure.

Scurrying back to the house as fast as I could, I let myself in the side door and came to a screeching halt in the hallway.

I had *no* idea where I was going.

A long hallway extended to my left, lined with suits of armor and closed doors. To the right, it seemed like it was more of the same except for an ornate clock set on an end table.

The clock seemed familiar, so I headed in that direction. Looping around the perimeter of the house, I walked straight into a formal living room or something that basically served as a dead end.

"So much for that," I muttered, trudging back the way I came.

I wandered for what felt like hours, opening the unlocked doors and giving the rooms cursory glances before moving on. I mean, seriously. How many parlors or sitting rooms or whatever the hell they were called did one person actually need? Gerulf said he wanted his laptop, which meant it was probably in the library or an office or something. Maybe even his bedroom, although *that* was an area I was definitely steering clear of. He'd probably throw me out a window for real if he caught me in his bedroom. I wasn't sure I remembered where the master bedroom was, anyway. It wasn't exactly the focal point of Gilroy's whirlwind tour of the house last night. Instead, he motioned down a hallway and said, "Mr. Prince's quarters are in this wing," and promptly took me to the *opposite* end of the house to show where I would be staying—in an opulent guest suite, which was probably the nicest accommodation I'd ever slept in. For some reason, I pictured myself sleeping in the attic like a scullery maid for the next six months, but even the regular staff had pretty nice rooms from the glances I got while meandering around on my own.

By some miracle, I made it back to the library on the ground floor.

One of the maids was inside dusting, humming along to herself as she ran a feather duster along the tops of the antique books.

"Excuse me?" I cleared my throat and took a step closer.

She stole a glance at me but didn't stop cleaning. "Oui?"

"'We'? Oh, right. You must be Lisette." She was the only member of the household staff I hadn't met the night before because, according to Mrs. Potter's excited whisper, she was on a date. Before she could divulge anything else, Gilroy came into the room, putting an end to the conversation.

Remembering my manners, I took another step forward

and extended my hand, retracting it again when she simply held up the duster as an excuse for not shaking. "Sorry. I'm Zane. I'm Gerulf's new assistant."

"Can I help you with something?" she asked, her voice accented but not entirely unfriendly. If anything, she sounded as bored with me as she was dusting hundreds, if not thousands, of books. Books that were woefully uncategorized—I learned that yesterday after my interview while I waited to meet the famous Gerulf Prince. Even now, my palms itched to reorganize everything into a proper system. How was anyone supposed to find the book they were looking for when the categories were all jumbled together? Not to mention the priceless first editions sharing shelf space with contemporary literature.

"Uh, yeah. Actually. Mr. Prince told me to bring him his laptop."

That got her to stop dusting, only to arch a blonde eyebrow at me. "His what?"

"Laptop?" I pantomimed typing, hoping it would help. "Computer?"

"I don't know what you're talking about."

"Portátil? Shit, that's Spanish. I'm sorry." I winced at the mistake. Then again, how different could romance languages be? Maybe she'd pick up what I was saying regardless.

Her pouty red lips pursed together and she propped a hand on the curve of her hip. "I know what a laptop is. I'm saying he doesn't have one."

"Then what does he use to write his books?"

"A typewriter," she replied with a smirk. Giving me a once-over, a look somewhere between pity and annoyance crossed her face. She shook her head at whatever her silent conclusion about me was and went back to dusting, flicking the feathers to and fro.

"A typewriter. Great. That's just... great." Of *course* he

used a typewriter. He probably wrote with fountain pens too. From everything I'd read online and everything I'd already seen with my own eyes, Gerulf was a pretentious snob with more money than he knew what to do with. Unlike most authors, he had the ability to use vintage items and writing methods because he had the ultimate luxury: time.

I raked a hand through my hair and pushed the mass of curls away from my face. Struck with an idea, I hurried over to the bell pull by the fireplace and gave it a tug.

Moments later, Gilroy appeared. He glanced around the library with a furrowed brow before turning his attention to me. "Was there something you needed, Mr. Beaumont?"

"Do you know where Gerulf keeps his typewriter?"

"His office, sir."

"Can you please point me in that direction?"

"I shall take you myself." He pivoted on his heel and walked out.

I hurried after him, following him down the hallway and trying to memorize the way as we walked.

"How are you adjusting to your new role?" Gilroy asked, his hands clasped primly behind his back.

"Well, he'd rather starve than eat in the same room as me, he tried to strangle me in the garden, and he told me to fetch a laptop that doesn't exist. I'd say things are going great," I muttered. While Gilroy wasn't as chatty as Mrs. Potter, I had a feeling he could still commiserate after his literal run-in with Gerulf yesterday.

Gilroy chuckled quietly. "You've lasted longer than the others, I'll give you that." He stopped in front of a closed door and gestured toward it. "It's on the desk."

"Great. Thank you. Is there a tray or something I can borrow? He's in the garden."

Gilroy regarded me for a moment and inclined his head. "I'll be right back."

As soon as Gilroy returned with a large wooden tray, I took it with a smile and expressed my gratitude before stepping into Geruf's office.

"Ok, asshole," I muttered to myself, hefting the antique typewriter off the desk and setting it on the tray, along with a stack of blank paper, a notebook, and a couple of pens (surprisingly *not* fountain) to be on the safe side. "I can play your game."

By the time I schlepped all of his stuff out to the garden, I fully expected Gerulf to be gone, to have come back up to the house or disappeared farther into the gardens since he knew I was on a fool's errand. Surprisingly, he was still on the same bench where I left him. The paper wrapping, I noted, was balled up and the thermos was actually in his hands.

"Did you find it?" Gerulf asked, lifting the metal cup to his lips as if it would hide his smirk. He didn't even bother looking in my direction. Smarmy bastard.

"Sure did," I replied with an acidic smile if he happened to glance my way. He didn't—not until I stopped directly in front of him and he was suddenly eye-level with the typewriter. "Where would you like it?"

He recoiled from the machine in his face before letting his gaze drift upward to mine. I still couldn't tell what color, exactly, his right eye was. It could have been blue *or* green. Either way, it was pale and icy, but ringed by a shocking dark teal around the outside. Contrary to what he probably thought, the loss of his left eye didn't make him any more intimidating than he would have been with both eyes intact. And it certainly didn't make him a monster.

In answer to my question, Gerulf slowly tossed his head to the side, indicating the empty bench next to him.

I gave him a curt nod and set the tray down. "Now what?"

"Feel free to scamper back to wherever it is you came from, kid. You're not needed."

"I'm twenty-five." I crossed my arms, realizing a second too late it completely undermined my rebuttal. Rather than uncross my arms and risk looking even more petulant, I held my ground. Unfortunately, I was used to being dismissed; people had been doing it my whole life for one reason or another. I was too scrawny, too pretty, too nerdy, too everything a boy *shouldn't* be by society's standards. Age (and height) helped somewhat, but the point of the matter was that I was used to proving myself to people who didn't think much of me. So if Gerulf thought he was going to run me off with a few snarky comments and waste my time, he had another thing coming.

"Do you know how many books I'd written by the age of twenty-five?" he asked, cocking his head.

"Published or unpublished?" I shot back.

The corner of his mouth lifted in another smirk. "How many books have *you* written?"

"None. Yet."

"Uh huh." He dragged his gaze down my body, pausing at my feet before darting up, like he was measuring my worth through sight alone, much like Lisette had done. "And yet you seem to think you're somehow qualified to help me with mine?"

"Your lawyer seems to think I'm qualified."

"My lawyer is an idiot."

"You hired him." Good one, Zane. Stoop to his level *and* insult him. That would surely win him over.

Gerulf set the thermos to the side and got to his feet slowly, fixing me with a pointed look. Considering me from head-to-toe again, he gave me a wide berth as he sidestepped me and moved down the garden path, leaving everything on the stone bench.

I bit my lip, cursing him silently. Why did someone so brilliant have to be such a fucking asshole? Would it kill him to be civil? Exhaling a slow, steady breath, I tossed the crumpled wrapper onto the tray and wedged the thermos next to the typewriter.

"Are you coming or not?" Gerulf's voice called out.

When I looked up, I was surprised to see he was watching me from across the garden. Not so surprising was the scowl plastered on his face.

Snatching a pen and notebook, I stuffed them both in my back pocket and hurried after him before he suddenly changed his mind and told me to beat it.

I'd barely caught up to him when he resumed walking. Well, limping. It wasn't noticeable with each step, but every so often he'd wince and his hand would drift to his left thigh, clutching it. I let it go the first couple of times, but eventually I blurted out, "Should we take a break?"

"You can't be tired already," he replied, walking onward, his back ramrod straight despite the way he favored his left side.

"I'm not, I just thought... I don't know. We've been walking for almost an hour and you haven't said anything."

"What does my silence have to do with your lack of endurance?" He arched an eyebrow to punctuate his condescending retort.

"I don't—" I blew out a breath. There was no way in hell I was going to point out my concern for his well-being when he was being so stubborn. And mean. He definitely didn't have to turn around and make everything so damn personal. "Why did you want me to come with you if you weren't going to talk?"

"Can't handle the thoughts in your own head? Is that why you don't like silence?" Oh my God! I was going to kill him. An hour ago, he was the one strangling me in the middle of a rose garden and now I was on the verge of strangling him by the row of neatly trimmed boxwoods.

"Listen," I said as calmly as I could, "I am *trying* here. I'm not some freeloader, ok? I *want* to help you. That is what I'm being paid to do. So if you want to use me as a whipping boy for six months, then fine. But spell it out for me so I know what to expect. Otherwise, we're both going to be spinning our wheels and for what? I'm sure we both have better things to do with our time than snipe at each other."

He finally stopped and turned halfway so he could look at me, his head tilted in thought. "You're a strange individual, you know that?"

"Look who's talking," I shot back.

"Tell me. Was being insubordinate on your list of qualifications?"

"Maybe if you'd bothered to look at my resume, you'd know the answer to that."

"I don't 'bother' to look at much of anything these days. Too much strain," he replied icily. "So why don't you dazzle me with a recitation of your illustrious achievements? The last time I checked my hearing was perfect."

"I majored in English Lit at the University of Chicago and then got my master's in Library Science. Graduated with honors, both times, *while* working to put myself through school. No, I haven't published a book, but I've had short stories published in literary magazines and anthologies across the world. And yes, one of these days I will get to my novel, but that's the least of my concerns right now."

"I'm positively awestruck." Gerulf sniffed and pivoted on his foot, carrying on down the garden path. As soon as I caught up to him again, he continued dismissing my entire existence in his eloquent—read: arrogant—manner. "Though I *am* curious about one thing, as much as it pains me to admit. What is your grand strategy in waiting to work on your manuscript? Going to write it all in your head before you bother putting it on paper? Or is it some pipe dream you've concocted to make yourself feel better about your current situation? I can't even tell you how many people talk about writing a book and yet so few of them actually managed to pull it off. But, of course, you're not *like* other people, right? You're *special*."

I made a conscious effort to unclench my jaw when I answered. Though I suppose it was easy for him to be haughty when he had a Pulitzer on his mantel and I most certainly did not. "There *is* no strategy. I don't have time right now."

"That's nothing but an excuse."

"A bit hypocritical, don't you think?"

"Oh, I have the time, as you can see. Plenty of time."

"Then what's *your* excuse? Hmm? Since you're the expert, why isn't *your* book finished?"

"Because I don't want to fucking write it." He sliced a glare at me out of the corner of his good eye, the icy bluish-green color almost as pale as the scarred one on the left.

I'm sure it was meant as a warning to shut up, but I kept going regardless. If it was something truly personal, I wouldn't have pried, but since it related to my job, I figured it might be helpful. Besides, he didn't care about trying to be civil, so why should I? "Why not? What's wrong with it?"

"I would ask you if you're writing a book with all of these questions, but I already know the answer is 'No.'" God, even his smile was sarcastic. Stunning and derisive all at once. Like the roses he seemed so fond of—beautiful, but full of thorns.

I gave up mimicking his shitty attitude. If I was ever going to get through to him, I needed to stop playing his juvenile games and trying to match him tit-for-tat. He was obviously far more experienced at it than I was. Maybe if I focused solely on the work, he'd realize I *was* a professional and I *was* trying to help. "Why don't you tell me what it's about? Maybe I can help with a plot hole or something."

For a moment, he actually looked disappointed that I

didn't rise to his challenge. I figured he was going to go back to ignoring me, but after another minute, he actually answered, minus the causticness. "It's supposed to be a psychological domestic thriller set in Chicago in the 1890s. Wealthy family. Murder, betrayal. The usual."

Well, *that* didn't sound like the basis of an award winner like everyone claimed. But, as with every book, the execution mattered more than the simplicity of the trope, so I wasn't going to give up on it yet. Especially since it was *Gerulf Prince* we were talking about, Asshole Author Extraordinaire, the man who could write a bestseller on a napkin if he was inspired to do so.

"Who's the murderer?" I asked.

He shrugged, staring out ahead of us and giving me absolutely nothing to work with.

"Ok... Who is the victim?"

"Some guy. I don't know. Haven't figured it out."

"So why is he murdered? For money? Revenge? Power?" I was grasping at straws here, and when he shrugged again, I wanted to shake him. "You had to have written down *something* for the publisher. Everyone has been buzzing about this book for years. What was the original idea you pitched to them? Or do they just write you a check carte blanche because you're Gerulf Prince?"

He stole a glance at me and I noticed the smirk back on his lips, like he knew how frustrated I was. Maybe, deep down, he shared the same frustration but because of who he was he'd never be able to admit he was struggling. He probably *did* have carte blanche to write whatever he wanted, but in the eyes of his business associates, it had better be a smash hit. Talk about killing your creativity.

"Ok," I sighed, gesturing with my hands to wipe the metaphorical slate clean. "Forget that. What's with the title? How's that related to the story?"

"No idea."

"Then why did you pick it?"

"I can't remember. And people only know about the damn thing because Faye leaked it, thinking the pressure would make me write faster. Shows how much she knows about my process." He snorted. "Or cares."

I quickly ran through the list of other employees at the house, but came up blank. "Who's Faye?"

His quiet laugh was closer to a snarl. "My fucking agent and former fiancée."

"Oh." Well, that must have been awkward... And I'm sure it did not help his current situation *at all.*

"So, do you finally see? I don't need your help because there *is* no book. This project has been cursed from the get-go." Coming to an abrupt halt, he faced me with wide eyes. "Cursed!"

"Cursed?" I blinked at him, trying to connect the dots in my head.

"Give me. Give me the pen." He waved impatiently at my hip. I glanced down to where the notebook was sticking out of my back pocket and did as he asked, handing the items over with a furrowed brow. He snatched them out of my grip and started scribbling immediately.

"Get an idea?"

Gerulf waved me away before turning and continuing on his walk. He was still writing, muttering to himself like a crazy person about people I didn't know and situations I didn't understand.

I wasn't sure if I should follow him or stay where I was. With the way he favored his left leg, I felt like I couldn't leave. Yet, he most definitely shooed me away like a gnat.

In the end, I opted to return to the rose garden and wait for him there. He'd have to pass by on his way back to the house, so I figured it was a good spot to hover. And if he fell, or needed help or something, maybe I'd hear him yell.

About an hour later, Gerulf appeared on the garden path, *still* writing as he walked. He paused now and again to apparently argue with himself before burying his nose in the notebook, the pen darting back and forth over the page.

"Bring the typewriter," he said on the way by, not even slowing down.

I scrambled to my feet and grabbed the tray, hurrying after him. Whatever limp he'd had was practically gone and he disappeared with far more speed than I would have anticipated from a man in his condition.

Maybe this was a good thing, though. Maybe this little burst of creative energy meant the next six months wouldn't be so terrible after all.

Chapter Six

GERULF

The following morning, Zane's brown puppy eyes widened when I slapped a notebook on the dining room table next to him, nearly upending his cup of tea in its saucer.

"Type that, and when you're finished, come find me," I said, pointing at the notebook in question.

He reached for it slowly, like it might bite him, and thumbed through the spent pages. "This was a brand new notebook."

"Yeah. And?"

Tucking a long, brown curl behind his ear, he went back to the beginning of my messy scrawl and settled in, apparently content to read right there instead of waiting until he was finished with breakfast. "These aren't just notes. This is... this is a story."

I couldn't help but roll my eyes. "Glad to see that master's degree really paid off."

Zane frowned up at me but refrained from further comment. Considering how feisty he was yesterday, I was surprised he didn't snap back with something about the fact I besmirched his intelligence. Surprised and a little disappointed, honestly. I wasn't sure if I needed that back-and-forth banter with another fairly clever person to get my brain working, but it *had* drummed up some inspiration, so I wasn't altogether opposed to trying again.

Since I couldn't do anything else until he did his part with the typing, I left the dining room and retreated to the library for some solitude while I plotted out the next couple of chapters.

That's where Zane found me a few hours later, a stack of typed pages in his hand. He held them out to me with a blank expression, but I didn't miss the way he fidgeted as he stood on the opposite side of the antique desk, picking at the hem of his t-shirt.

"What?" I huffed, knowing I'd probably regret it in two seconds.

"Nothing."

I stared at him, head cocked, waiting for the real answer.

"I think you should change the villain," he said in a rush, pinkness immediately flooding his pale cheeks.

"I'm not paying you to critique it," I replied, tossing the pages on the desk and leaning back in my chair, meeting his gaze head-on.

"No, you're paying me to help you. And I'm telling you, the villain would be much stronger as a woman."

My brow furrowed as I contemplated the point. I wasn't averse to the idea, but I needed more from him—a valid reason to make the change as opposed to shaking things up for the novelty of it. "Why?"

"Because no one ever suspects them," he replied with a small shrug, his gaze darting away as he spoke. "Society severely underestimates their capacity for evil or they shrug it off and make excuses for them. Leave red herrings for the first guy, Neal, like you already have. But July? The maid? Make her the real killer. It's a better plot twist because we're all taught to view women as nurturing, not harmful."

A feather could have knocked me over with the realization he was right. On more than one account. Why didn't I make the connection sooner? *Me.* Of all damn people! Lord knows I had plenty of experience being painted as the villain when the real malefactor sat idly by with a smug smile. And from the way Zane shrank inside of himself while talking, I had a sinking feeling he also had first-hand knowledge of being victimized by the fairer sex.

He must have taken my silence for disbelief because the next thing I knew, he hurried to my side and angled the papers toward himself, flipping through them quickly. "It's not going to take much revision, I promise. You've already laid the groundwork. See here?" He pointed out a passage as he spoke. "She's spiteful and vicious and hates the Chandlers. She serves them because she has to, but in her mind, she's superior. When the footman pointed out her lack of education and manners? Look how she reacted. She's vile, even though she tries to hide it."

"Thank you. Now get out," I murmured, my mind already whirling with new possibilities as I took the stack of papers from him.

The warmth in his brown eyes disappeared. "But I—"

"What? Are you going to stand there and stare at me while I write?"

"Well, no, but—"

"Then get out."

Huffing, he frowned at me. "I was wondering if you'd like me to catalog the library for you."

"No, I wouldn't."

"It would be a better use of my time," he continued, unfazed by my answer. "Instead of paying me to sit here and wait for you to finish another chapter, I could do a complete inventory of the books, which is good for your insurance, and set up a proper cat—"

"Out!" I pointed at the door to emphasize the order and turned my attention to the pages, uncapping a red pen to signal I was done with the conversation.

Scribbling on both sides of the typed manuscript, I started making amendments and added bits of foreshadowing where I could. As I worked, I couldn't ignore the weight of Zane's gaze on me as he made his way to the door with the speed of a snail. If he was looking for a pat on the head for his contribution to the book or his attempt at being helpful with the library, he wasn't going to get it. I had a fucking book to write and I couldn't afford to be distracted any more than I'd already been.

As the days wore on, we fell into a similar pattern. I would write by hand and deliver the pages to Zane to transcribe so I could edit easily. He would return them to me as soon as he was done and then stand around, shuffling his feet, waiting for me to practically beat his opinion out of him. When he wasn't staring at me like a nervous puppy, he gazed longingly at the books all around us with his hands clasped, as if he had to hold himself back from touching them. It was kind of endearing to watch, even if did ultimately disrupt my editing time.

One day, however, he set the stack of papers on my desk and let his fingers drift across the center reverently, offering his unsolicited thoughts with an equally awed tone. "I'm sure you're used to hearing it by now, but this is brilliant, Gerulf. Just... brilliant."

"What are you talking about?" I made a face at him, dragging the typed pages closer. My hand grazed over his in the process and once again I was surprised at how warm his skin was. How soft. Everything about him was so gentle, I doubted he'd ever hit anything in anger in his entire life or even raised his voice.

Zane retreated to the far side of the desk, taking his hand with him and flexing it at his side. "This. This story. These characters. The darkness is... insidious. When I first heard what you were planning for this book, I thought it was going to be violent in an overt sense, in a way that we're used to. But this is worse. It poses the question: what do you do when you don't even feel safe in your own home? Where do you go? And what happens when that evil follows you? I think the domestic violence angle is going to resonate with people more than they realize because it creeps up on you, like in real life. Before you know it, you're trapped."

"You're just happy I made July the killer." I arched a brow at him, daring him to deny it.

A flush spread across his cheeks and he looked away. "I mean, I stand by that suggestion. I think it's part of what makes this book so good. Because it's unexpected. But it speaks to a larger issue." When his gaze returned to mine and actually lingered, a strange sensation fluttered through my chest, quickening my heartbeat.

Pride. I'm sure that's all it was. It was the satisfaction found in receiving a compliment—a genuine compliment from a flesh-and-blood person as opposed to critics' and bloggers' sycophantic praise. A compliment from someone who had read hundreds, if not thousands, of books. Someone who made it their mission to inspire a love of reading in others. Someone who had no idea where this story was going but was already confident of its ultimate success. Of *my* ultimate success.

I cleared my throat, forcing my attention to the stack of fresh pages in front of me instead of trying to determine, once and for all, what shade of brown his eyes were. I was torn between umber and cinnamon, anyway. "Thank you. You can—"

"Get out. I know," he said with a definitive nod, his disappointment palpable.

"I was going to say 'stay.' Only if you want," I added quickly when his brow furrowed. "I know you've been dying to properly catalog the library and God knows it needs it. But, like I said, only if you want. It's not part of your contract so you're under no obligation to if you've changed your mind. I know it's a lot of work."

His lips curved into a small, wary smile and his gaze was full of suspicion, like he was waiting for me to yank the proverbial rug out from under his feet. "You mean it? You actually want my help with the library?"

"Yes. I do. But try to keep it down. Please. I, um, have this. To do." I picked up my pen and tapped the manuscript rather than slapping myself for rambling on like an idiot. "I can't be distracted and noise is distracting." Eloquent, Gerulf. Real fucking eloquent.

"You won't even know I'm here. I promise." Zane pressed his hands together in barely contained happiness and backed away from me slowly, like he was removing himself from the presence of royalty. Once he was a few steps away, he spun on the ball of his foot and practically sprinted to the far end of the library, his chestnut curls bouncing on his shoulders with each step.

He could promise all he wanted, but it wouldn't stop me from glancing up every other sentence, seeking him out, and taking note of whatever he was doing—the way his willowy frame moved with ease, how his soft laughter was irritatingly infectious, or the fact each and every thought he had was mirrored in the expressions on his face.

"Focus," I hissed at myself, dragging the papers closer and forcing my gaze downward to the task at hand instead of watching Zane float around the library like he was on Cloud Nine.

I couldn't help it, though. The more I was in his presence, the more I found myself entranced by him. Whether Zane realized it or not, I'd been struggling with the main character in *Loss of Twilight* and had yet to nail down his personality. I hoped it would reveal itself as the story wore on, as some characters had the tendency to do, but the perfect source of inspiration was literally right in front of me. Someone readers could empathize with, someone they would be invested in. More importantly, someone they could love. Someone exactly like Zane.

My head canted to one side, watching my assistant across the room. He was up on the rolling ladder, sorting through books on the top shelf. I couldn't see what title he had in his hand, but whatever it was made him smile and steal a glance in my direction.

Another flutter in my chest had me exhaling sharply. Even from a distance, the warmth of his smile enveloped me. He looked away quickly, gathered a stack of books in one arm, and descended the ladder again.

"Perfect," I whispered to myself. Taking one last look at Zane's pink-tinged cheeks before he used his curls to shield his face like a curtain, I picked up my pen again and got to work.

Chapter Seven

ZANE

Per the contract, Sundays were supposed to be my one guaranteed day off, but given the fact I was perpetually on thin ice with Gerulf, I didn't push it by trying to leave the estate the first three months I was there. Knowing how much he generally despised my existence, I didn't want to give him any reason to fire me, even if I hadn't been able to see my dad in person during that whole time. The nurses FaceTimed me, but it wasn't the same.

When Mrs. Potter announced that Gerulf would be gone for lunch one Sunday, I was ecstatic. I finally had a day I could sneak out to the hospital! My happy bubble burst when Gerulf appeared a little while later and said I needed to drive him into the city. Needless to say, I was less than thrilled about the change of plans but I went and got the car anyway. It's not like I could really say "No." Besides, I was more irritated with the fact I wanted to be in the city anyway—just not with my boss.

Perceptive as ever, in the seconds it took me to nod glumly in acquiescence to his request, Gerulf's good eye narrowed and he stepped closer. The space between us filled with the spicy scent of his expensive cologne and I did my best to ignore it, but it was impossible. It was like ignoring Gerulf himself. Even if he'd turned into a grouchy hermit, his presence was still larger-than-life, commanding your attention.

"Is that a problem for you?" he asked, his voice low.

I shook my head mutely. Papa would understand why I wasn't there, if he could understand anything anymore. At this point, I was sure the visits were more for me than for him, anyway.

Apparently, I wasn't convincing enough, since Gerulf brought it up again as we got on the tollway, headed east-bound in his black BMW.

"Any other time I ask you to do something, you do it without hesitation," Gerulf said. "You even volunteer to take on *more* work than is required of you, such as the library. Today, all I asked is that you drive a car to a city you used to live in and you're acting like I kicked a puppy right in front of you. But please, continue to brood with no explanation."

I tightened my grip on the steering wheel, trying to figure out the best way to phrase it without leading to more questions. "I thought I would have the day off today. That's all."

"Why? Did you have plans?"

"Maybe."

"Doing what?"

"It doesn't matter."

"I'd beg to differ. It seems to matter very much, considering how sullen you look."

"I'm not sullen."

"And now you're defensive. Not to mention the fact you're being vague with your answers. Usually, you give me a dissertation in response to a question and now all you're giving me are basic syllables. Should I expect you to start grunting next?"

"Do you scrutinize everyone this way?" I stole a glance at

him out of the corner of my eye, not the least bit surprised to see he was watching me like a hawk. He always did. Whenever I was within his line of sight, it was like I could feel his gaze taking in every detail, every movement, no matter how small. At first, it was unnerving and I fully expected to be fired at a moment's notice for whatever mistake he'd inevitably catch. Then I started recognizing traits of myself in his main character as I transcribed the manuscript. After that, I was simultaneously flattered and even more confused about where I stood with him. He acted like he hated me and yet the descriptions in his book cast me (well, his main character, *obviously*) in a shining light. He was a brilliant writer, without question, but still... I highly doubted he'd be inspired to wax poetically about someone he was perpetually irritated by, so I must have been doing something right despite all his cutting remarks and snappy comebacks.

"Only the people living in my house," Gerulf replied matter-of-factly, bringing me right back to the argument and serving as a perfect example of him being annoyed simply by the fact I was breathing the same air as him.

"I've never heard you question Mrs. Potter like this."

"Because Mrs. Potter doesn't lie to me."

I scoffed and rolled my eyes. I wouldn't say "lie" was the right word, but she and Gilroy seemed to treat Gerulf more like their child than their employer—meaning they placated him and omitted upsetting truths, like trying to soothe a toddler on the verge of a tantrum. All in the name of keeping his blood pressure and his pain levels down, or so they told me. The whole house catered to his every whim, but those two went above and beyond to make his life as comfortable and stress-free as they could.

"I'm not lying," I huffed after a minute, giving up on trying to keep my personal life to myself. "I wanted to see my dad today. That's it. That's my big plan for the day. Happy?"

"To do what?"

"Oh my God." I shot him another look. "What does it matter?"

He shrugged. "Just wondering what a twenty-something wants to do with their father on a Sunday that has him so crabby."

"First of all, you're one to talk about crabbiness. You're like the king crab. Second of all, it's none of your business. I told you the truth, but I don't have to tell you everything. So picture whatever you did with your dad and there you go."

"I didn't do anything with my dad."

"What?"

"My father was too busy to 'do' things. He was always working. And then he died."

"What about your mom?"

"Dead." He leveled an unamused look at me, though his voice was seemingly unaffected by the heaviness of the conversation. "Want to ask about my grandparents?"

"No, I get the drift," I replied, adding, "I'm sorry," after a few moments. "My mom died too."

We fell into silence after that. It wasn't entirely uncomfortable, but I also didn't feel the need to break up the uneasiness by asking any more questions. I trusted he'd tell me where we were going the closer we got to Chicago. And he did.

He directed me to a vast medical complex surprisingly near my dad. Like, on the opposite end of the exact hospital I'd been planning on going to. Given his injuries, it made sense Gerulf would be going somewhere that specialized in trauma and recovery.

"I shouldn't be long," Gerulf said when the car rocked to a stop in the circular drive outside a surgeon's office. Tugging up the hood on his black zip-up sweatshirt, he stole a glance at his watch. "Maybe an hour."

"Do you mind if I go over to the hospital side? You can text me when you're done and I'll be right back."

"Are you ill?"

"No..." Shit! I shouldn't have said anything. I should have just gone and made sure to come back before he was done and then this whole conversation would have never even happened. So much for trying to keep my personal life personal.

"Then why are you going to the hospital?"

"You're not going to let this go, are you?"

He made no move to get out of the car and simply stared at me with his usual intensity, like he had X-ray vision straight into my soul.

"My dad's a patient there," I mumbled, gripping the steering wheel tighter and refusing to look at him.

"Why couldn't you just say that?"

"Because I didn't want to get into it with you, ok? You already hate me. I don't need to give you any more ammunition or have you questioning my dedication to this job."

"I don't hate you."

"Well, you don't really like me," I said, finally letting my gaze slide to his.

He considered it for a moment before shrugging, an upside-down smile on his face. I thought maybe he was going to keep arguing or at least half-heartedly attempt to try and convince me I was mistaken. Nope. Without another word, Gerulf opened the car door and got out, closing the door on my incredulous scoff.

"He's unbelievable. Absolutely un-fucking-believable." Rolling my eyes, I pulled away from the curb and circled around the outside of the hospital.

Aside from the past few months, I'd been here so often I could make the trip blindfolded. Through the lobby, make a quick stop at the gift shop, up the elevator, and two right-turns to get to where I needed to be.

"Hi Papa," I said as I entered. Only the usual whirring and beeping sounds greeted me in return. I pulled the withered bouquet out of the vase by his bed and tossed it in the trash. The inside of the vase had gotten all scummy since the last time I sent flowers, so I gave it a cursory rinse in the sink before refilling it and arranging the fresh roses.

"I'm sorry I haven't been around a lot lately," I said, leaning over to kiss Papa's forehead, mindful of the scarred skin on his face, before easing into the chair next to him.

"This new job has taken up more of my time than I originally thought it would, which I guess is both good and bad. I'm actually learning a lot about what it takes to be an author. It's not as glamorous as people probably think it is. I'm pretty sure helping you file patents was easier." Running my palms over my knees, I settled back in the chair, trying to fool myself into thinking this was a casual chat at home and not where we actually were.

"You won't even believe who I'm working for, though," I continued. "I can hardly believe it sometimes. Gerulf Prince! You know, the guy who wrote *Outside the Storm.* I think that was the only book I could get you to read that one summer. Then you wouldn't stop talking about it." I shook my head at the memory, chuckling, until it faded to a sigh.

"But I hate to break it to you, Papa, he's an asshole. I mean, maybe he hasn't always been, but he certainly is now. I guess you can understand what he's going through. Accidents tend to change people...

"His house is amazing, though. It's like a palace. And he's *so* smart. He's kind of like you, actually. Out of nowhere, he gets these random ideas, and then bam! He's off and running and I can barely keep up. He writes everything by hand now and I do the typing for him, since he can't do it himself anymore.

"There's something really interesting about seeing his thoughts come out on the paper, like when he scratches out words and rewrites stuff, or when his writing gets sloppy because he's going so quick. It's a totally different side of him than what he presents in person. It's like writing is the only time he lets himself express any emotion, unless it's some version of being pissed off. *That* he has no problem expressing. I thought it would make him happier, though, to be writing again. Sometimes I think he's going through the motions, but I don't know if his heart is necessarily in this story. Maybe because it's been so long since he started it and there's so much hype around it. Maybe he's *not* an asshole and he's just anxious or insecure or something.

"I don't know," I sighed, blowing off my own observation. "I'm no one. Literally, no one. I don't know anything about what it takes to be a real author, let alone one at his level. Maybe after all this time he doesn't get excited about writing anymore. It's like any other job. He does it, gets paid, and moves on. And I'm the idiot who romanticizes the whole process."

I steered the conversation away from Gerulf and told Papa about Mrs. Potter and Gilroy and all of the other servants at Gerulf's house; how incredibly inviting they'd been, as if they were trying to make up for our employer's never-ending brusqueness. I talked about books and the weather, any random topic to fill the silence and let him know I was there, in case he could hear me somewhere inside his coma. And once again, I somehow circled back around to Gerulf.

"I don't know what else to do, Papa. I really want to impress him, but I'm starting to think that's impossible. He doesn't seem to care that I'm cataloging his library for him—at no additional cost, I might add. I don't even know if he likes the system I put into place. After I started moving the books around, I walked in one day and saw him staring at one of the new sections, so I asked if he was looking for a certain book and he didn't even answer me. Literally, zilch. He opened his mouth, looked at me, looked at the books, and then marched out of the library. I didn't see him again until dinner and there was *no* way I was going to ask any follow-up questions. But then the way he's basically written me into *Loss of Twilight*...

"God, he's probably the most frustrating person I've ever met!" Shifting forward with a groan, I propped my elbows on my knees and buried my face in my hands. "I wish you were here to give me some advice on how to win him over."

"Are you about finished?" a voice asked from the doorway. Not just any voice. Geruf's voice, gruff and unamused as always.

Bolting upright, I looked in horror at the door. I desperately hoped it was a figment of my imagination, but no. It was indeed Gerulf, leaning against the doorframe, hood up and arms crossed. He stared at me with a blank expression, giving zero indication if he'd heard me or not.

"Fuck..." I squeezed my eyes shut and opened them again with a grimace. "How long have you been standing there?"

"Long enough." Double fuck.

"You said it was going to be an hour," I said, swallowing my nerves in preparation for an ass-chewing or my impending termination.

"It was going to be, but that was before I told Roger to fuck off and left."

"The surgeon?" I gaped at him. "The surgeon who made a special appointment for you on the weekend so you could avoid people? You told him to 'fuck off'? Just like that?"

Unperturbed, Gerulf nodded. "Yeah. Just like that." His attention moved from me to my father, though his face remained devoid of any expression. Pushing off the doorframe, he made his way closer to the bed, examining the tubes and wires. "What happened to him?"

"There, um, was an explosion. At his workplace. He's an inventor. I mean, an engineer. Whatever. Anyway, he was down on the production floor working on some prototype. I guess there was a buildup of gas or something in the air and all it took was one spark from static electricity." I glanced between my father and Gerulf, wondering what he was thinking.

The similarity between them wasn't just the fascinating way their brains operated—their disfigurement was as clear as day. While Gerulf had angry, jagged scars, Papa was covered in burns. Practically every part of him had been caught in the blast.

The doctors put him in a coma to recover, and once he came out of it, they were supposed to begin the painful process of skin grafts. Except, he didn't. Nearly six months later and he still wasn't showing any signs of improvement. Even though they threw around terms like "persistent vegetative state" and talked about "brain stem reflexes," none of the doctors had the nerve to tell me what I already knew—my father was dead. The machines were the only thing keeping his body alive and it was going to be up to me to turn them off. Or whenever the insurance decided to quit paying for his care.

"I'm sorry," Gerulf said quietly, his gaze downcast and the muscles in his throat constricting. "I didn't realize you were dealing with this."

"We're all dealing with something, right?" I tried to crack a smile to lighten the oppressive weight in the room, but I'm pretty sure it looked more like a wince.

Clearing my throat, I got to my feet quickly and stuffed all of my emotions back inside where they belonged. Crying like a baby in front of my boss was *not* something I was prepared to do especially since I just admitted out loud that I was trying to win him over. I may have looked like a delicate flower, but I'd be damned if I acted like it.

I said goodbye to my dad and hurried out of the room, bracing for Round Two of Gerulf's interrogation. He stayed right behind me, each step of the way, remaining just outside of my peripheral vision. I don't know if it was his attempt to give me space or if he was purposely distancing himself in case he thought I was going to have a breakdown in public. Part of me expected him to at least try to say something optimistic in the privacy of the elevator or in the car on the way home.

He didn't.

He didn't because there was nothing optimistic *to* say. I knew the statistics; he probably did too. Injuries that bad? A coma that long? It was only a matter of time. Everyone knew it.

Little did I know that time would come the following morning.

Gerulf and I were sitting down to breakfast, his latest stack of papers and two pens between us so we could make amendments as we talked, when my cell phone rang.

"It's the hospital," I said, staring at the caller ID, a block of ice forming in the pit of my stomach. These days, they never called. They'd only done that when he was in the burn unit. Now that he was in long-term care, they reserved any updates for an email or when I contacted them because there usually *weren't* any. A phone call now, this early in the morning, could only mean one thing.

"Answer it," Gerulf said, glancing pointedly at the phone.

I shook my head and shoved it at him. "You do it."

"Zane, no! I—"

"Please? I can't." My lower lip was already trembling, along with the phone in my hand.

Relenting with a sigh, he set his fork down and took my phone, answering it before it went to voicemail. "No, it's not," he said, cutting a quick glance in my direction. "He's here, but indisposed. I can take a message and have him call you right—"

My throat seized and no amount of swallowing would get it to loosen. As soon as Gerulf's gaze dropped to his plate, I knew. I knew for certain. It was *the* call.

Pushing away from the table, I slapped a hand over my mouth to keep the sob inside and got to my feet. I stopped at the far end of the dining room, far enough away for privacy but still close enough to hear what Gerulf was saying.

I tried to keep my ragged breathing in check by staring out at the gardens beyond the window. It was a dull, gray day. Wind howled against the glass. The leaves outside were falling like snow, swirls of red and orange and yellow gusting over the ground. The gardens were mostly dormant, hunkering down for the coldest, darkest part of the year. I guess I was too—bracing for the coldest, darkest part of my life now that I was well and truly alone.

A warm, solid hand slid over my shoulder, hesitantly, as the smell of Gerulf's cologne wrapped me in a cocoon. After a moment, his grip tightened, giving a gentle squeeze. "I'm so sorry, Zane."

Tears slipped down my cheeks, but I didn't dare turn around. If I did, I'd probably end up sobbing hysterically on the floor for hours and I couldn't risk this job. Not now. Now that I had nothing else going for me, no one else to turn to, and not when we were in the middle of both the book and the library projects.

"If there's anything I can do... Or anything you need—"

"The food is getting cold," I said, dashing the tears away with the edge of my sleeve, the navy yarn disguising the dampness. "I know how much you despise cold eggs. And we have a busy day planned. There's a lot of work to do."

"Yeah. We do." Gerulf gave my shoulder another squeeze and retreated across the room with slow, measured steps.

I expelled a shaky breath and wiped my eyes again before rejoining him at the table. Funeral arrangements and assets and lawyers—all of it could wait another day. It would *have* to wait another day until I could come to terms with this new reality. It didn't matter that I'd known this moment was coming, how could anyone prepare for the suffocating wave of sorrow following the death of their parent?

Papa had always joked that books were my life, but it was never more true than in this moment when I had nothing else to cling to. Trivial as it was, helping Gerulf finish his manuscript gave me a reason to keep going. Finishing the library was a reason to get out of bed in the morning. Gerulf was a lifeline in a sea of uncertainty, a lighthouse to give me direction, when all I wanted to do was close my eyes and let the water swallow me whole. Even though I couldn't see myself talking to him about my grief when he'd experienced so much in his own life, I found solace in the fact he understood implicitly what I was going through.

Once upon a time, I'd cursed Gerulf for being such an insufferable asshole, and now, I thanked God I had him for my darkest day, even if I'd never tell him that. Ever. Not in a million lifetimes. I couldn't do anything that would remotely compromise my job here, which also meant I needed to squash the budding feelings that had taken root ever since I recognized myself in his main character.

There were a thousand reasons why crushing on your boss was a bad idea, but only one really mattered: in less than three months, I'd be gone and my heart couldn't take any more loss.

Chapter Eight

GERULF

“I think I can fit a couple more,” Zane said, dangling precariously on the rolling library ladder as he tried to wedge another book onto the top shelf.

“This is not how I typically spend New Year’s Eve, you know,” I said, looking up at him and trying to feign my exasperation. It wasn’t really that hard. My idea of ringing in the new year was to be tucked in bed by ten, leaving the celebratory nonsense to the rest of the world. I couldn’t really drink anymore because of all my medication and fireworks gave me a splitting headache, so what was there to celebrate?

Apparently, Zane’s idea of a good time was finishing his beloved enterprise in the library. It was finally cataloged to his satisfaction, despite my best efforts at stalling him over the last couple of weeks. I’d moved sections of books, deleted the master file of the catalog from his laptop, and even sabotaged the ladder’s wheel, all to no avail. He’d remedied each problem without even breaking a sweat—or questioning the odds of so many misfortunes happening so close together—and was now on his way to shelving the very last tome.

Over the last several weeks, with each book he re-shelved,

my unease grew stronger. Once the library project was finished, he'd have nothing else to keep him here. There was only one chapter left in *Loss of Twilight* and his contract was days away from terminating. Zane would go from a daily presence in my life to... nothing. A constant companion turned into a ghost. Ever since it dawned on me, the realization had left me with a strange heaviness in the center of my chest that I'd been lugging around, like Jacob Marley and his chains.

"You mean to tell me you don't have a private firework show for the staff and bust out your best champagne?" Zane grinned down at me from the top of the ladder, his face half-obscured by his crazy, curly hair. On the days his efforts were focused on the library, he pulled it back in a bun, but tonight he'd left it loose, indicating to me he hadn't planned on finishing this little pet project until Mrs. Potter oh-so-helpfully asked him how it was going over canapés.

"You think I'm going to pay you to sit around and drink all night?" I rolled my eyes.

"I thought for sure there'd at least be caviar and lobster at dinner and whatever else rich people eat."

"I'm sorry the prime rib wasn't up to your lavish standards."

"Oh, the prime rib was great compared to the risotto."

"You don't like truffles?"

"Yeah, the chocolate kind—not the ones that taste like dirt."

I scowled at him. "Do you have any idea how expensive those truffles were? I had the chef order them special for you" —I coughed and cleared my throat— "all. You all. The staff, I mean."

Thankfully he seemed oblivious to my near-slip, since he laughed and grabbed another book. Stretching farther on the ladder instead of doing the sensible thing, like moving it, he wriggled the book between two other volumes. "Should have saved your money."

"You realize when you fall, I'm not going to catch you, right?" Nevertheless, I tightened my grip on the ladder, hoping I had enough strength to at least keep it steady for him. He might have claimed he successfully fixed the broken wheel, but I wasn't entirely convinced.

"I'm sure that has more to do with your poor nerve endings and not your feelings toward me, right?" he replied with another grin.

"Considering you've been on my last nerve since the moment I met you, I'd say they're one and the same."

Laughing softly, he climbed down the ladder. I shifted to the side to make room for him but held on in case it tried to roll away at the last second. On his way down, his fingers grazed mine on one of the rungs. The movement was so quick, the barest trace of a touch, I wasn't sure if it had happened at all or if was just my imagination. That was until I looked at Zane's face. Crimson flared along both cheeks and he diverted his eyes. "Sorry."

"It's ok," I replied, watching him descend the rest of the way. Instead of walking away as soon as his feet hit the floor, he hung onto the side of the ladder, more or less mirroring my pose as I stood there. Arching an eyebrow, I watched as he chewed his lower lip in silence, turning it redder than it already was.

Shifting on his feet, he finally spoke, though he only managed to make eye contact every other word. "You know, I've been meaning to... I don't think I've ever properly thanked you."

"For what?"

"Making this time of year a little less lonely without my dad. I know you know what it's like, so I appreciate you helping me... adjust. To a new normal. Especially with the holidays. I know we kind of pretended they weren't happening and buried our heads in work, but I guess that's what it's going to be like from now on, huh? It's not like there's family to celebrate with."

"Well, we *did* have a lot of work to do. I mean, books don't write themselves. Plus you had to go and rearrange the whole library, so that took time. And, besides, I'm technically paying you to be here, so... It's not like I did you a favor or anything. It's business. Transactional. That's... all." Jesus, it was hot in here all of a sudden. Why did Gilroy feel the need to turn the heat all the way up *and* light the fireplaces? Then again, maybe it was the cashmere sweater I was wearing. I should have opted for a button-up instead.

The heat must have been getting to Zane too because his cheeks flushed deeper and he licked his lips. "Wow. Here I was trying to express my gratitude and you go and make me sound like some hooker you picked up downtown."

"If anything, I'd say it makes you more of an escort. You know, the whole companionship aspect? Unless you *were* planning on putting out before you leave... then that might qualify as prostitution. I'd have to look into it. The legalities of sex work aren't really my forte." Oh my God! Clearly, the filter between my brain and my mouth had ceased to function in the last ten seconds. I blamed the heat. It short-circuited something up there. Or maybe all the side effects of my medications were catching up to me, combined with the minuscule amount of wine we had with dinner in an effort to be festive.

Although the shocking part was the longer I thought about it, I kind of didn't care about my blundering banter. Flirting? Jesting. I'd call it jesting. As a rule, I did *not* flirt, even before the accident. It was an annoying game of cat and mouse and, as evidenced by the fact I basically called one of the kindest people I'd ever met a whore to his face, I wasn't good at it.

Regardless of whatever label applied to my verbal idiocy, I was struck with the sudden desire to see how scarlet Zane's skin could get. It had been an increasingly amusing pastime for me, especially after his father passed. In the days that followed that tragic phone call, I made a conscious effort to cut back on the curt remarks and dismissive tone and swapped it for *this*, giving him a hard time with enough sarcasm so he knew I was joking. To my delight, it worked! He still had moments of sadness, but for the most part, he went back to being the bright-eyed, pain in my ass he was on Day One, exuding an infectious warmth I couldn't seem to get enough of.

For his part, Zane was torn between laughing and sputtering out some sort of defense, looking anywhere *but* my face. "I mean... I don't recall reading *that* in the job description anywhere... I guess I'll have to look again."

"That wasn't a 'No.'" I watched his expression carefully, wondering when exactly I'd lost my mind and why I hoped he'd keep squirming like that, sinking his teeth into his lower lip.

"Well, it wasn't a 'Yes.'" Zane stole a glance at me, immediately looking away when he saw my gaze was still fixed on him.

"So it's a 'Maybe'?"

"It's a bad idea," he said softly, shifting his weight from one foot to the other and leaning against the ladder. No matter how hard I willed it, he refused to look at me, even after his hand accidentally slid into mine on the same ladder rung. "Whether you're being serious or speaking hypothetically."

A pang of rejection hit me right in the gut, harder than I thought was possible anymore. After the accident, I'd given up on the thought of being with anyone, let alone having someone *want* to be with me. But somehow the teasing had turned real. I took a chance, positing a genuine question under the guise of jest, and the rebuff sent heat prickling along the back of my neck. "Because of this?" I gestured vaguely to my face, already knowing the answer.

"Because you're my boss," he replied without even missing a beat. His gaze lifted to mine again, sadness lingering in his dark eyes. As he spoke, he only focused on my right eye, which lent some credibility to the fact he was downplaying my hideous appearance, even after I gave him an easy out. Either way, I couldn't blame him for not being attracted to someone so fucking damaged—in more ways than one. The scars ran deeper than my mangled flesh. Young though he was, Zane had enough sense to know that and he had the foresight to steer clear of men like me.

"I see." Blood pounded in my ears so hard I barely heard my own reply. I needed to leave, but my feet were frozen to the ground. Not to mention, my hand was still clutching the ladder rung, right next to his, heat radiating between our hands.

"I don't think you do." He paused, the corners of his eyes tightening. "I learned a long time ago not to want what I can't have. Professionalism aside, chasing straight guys never ends well for guys like me."

"Zane, I—"

The rest of my words came to a screeching halt as the library doors slammed open, banging against the dark wood paneling on the walls. The all-too-familiar sound of high heels clicking on the polished floors unleashed a tidal wave of fury inside of me.

Zane and I both turned toward the blonde bitch sauntering into the library like she owned the place, completely ignoring Gilroy who was hot on her heels, chewing her out for not waiting in the foyer like she'd been told.

Shedding her fur coat, Faye tossed it at Gilroy's face with a smirk. "Be a dear and hang that up."

My poor butler looked at me for further instructions, but

I was too enraged to speak, so I merely nodded. It's not that I wanted her to stay; if we knew where all her shit was, it would be easier to grab it all in one go and throw her out on her ass.

"Who's this?" Faye asked, setting her lecherous sights on Zane. "An intern? No, no. Not on a holiday. I'm guessing a caretaker. Right? Are you the new nurse who gets paid to put up with this hateful bastard?"

Before Zane could answer her ridiculous question, I stepped between them, as if it would somehow shield him from the toxicity she oozed with every breath. "He's no one as far as you're concerned. Want to tell me what the fuck you're doing here?"

"Still have a temper. What a surprise," Faye replied with a dazzlingly vicious smile. I couldn't help but notice one of the absurdly expensive bags I'd purchased for her was swinging from her elbow as she crossed her arms beneath her breasts, pushing them up even higher under her emerald dress, as if that trick still held any appeal. After all the shit she'd pulled over the years, she could have been on her knees begging me for it and I wouldn't touch her with a ten-foot pole and someone *else's* dick.

"I'll, just, um... yeah." Zane pointed at the door as he eased toward it. He exchanged a long look with Faye on his way by. She bit her lower lip suggestively; meanwhile, he made a face at her and quickened his steps. Gay or not, at least he was smart enough not to fall under the spell her beauty tended to cast over people. Smarter than me, anyway.

The minute Zane shut the door, she dropped the sex kitten act and rolled her eyes. "Don't act like you're not happy to see me." Her blonde hair shifted over her shoulder as she tilted her head, her lip curled. "Well, as much as you can see, anyway. Right, baby?"

Even though glaring didn't have any effect on her, I did it anyway, my hands instinctively balling at my sides. "Once again, Faye... What the fuck are you doing here?" I made sure to repeat it at an insultingly slow pace.

"Maybe if you'd pick up a phone once in a while, I wouldn't have had to come all the way out here. But since you couldn't do that and that worthless lawyer of yours is off on vacation, here I am with a little anniversary present for you." She shoved a hand into her purse and rummaged around, unearthing a massive stack of papers folded in half with a rubber band around them.

"I told you, stick to buying books, sweetheart. You don't have the talent for writing," I sneered at her. "That's why you dictate your emails, remember?"

Her shrill, mocking laugh was like an icepick in my eardrum. "Oh, Gerulf. Witty as ever. Glad to see that accident didn't fuck up your brain as much as your face."

"You fucking bitch."

"Save that fight for court, Ger." She smashed the papers into my chest and shoved me for good measure. "You're going to need it."

I didn't have to read beyond SUMMONS before my heart rate went into overdrive. "You're suing me?!"

"You're damn right I'm suing you!" Folding her arms over her chest, one hip popped to the side, as full of self-righteousness as ever. "The past two years have been hell for me! It's time you own up to your actions and pay for what you did."

Spiking the paperwork on the floor, I stepped over it to close the distance between us. "Hell for *you*?! Can you even hear yourself, you fucking narcissist?!"

"Oh, here we go. Trying to play the victim again?" She uncrossed her arms and shoved me in the chest even harder than before, rage darkening her face. "No one is going to buy that, Gerulf! No one! Everyone knows you lose your shit over every little thing! Throw in some alcohol and voila! Case closed. You can tell the court whatever you want, but no one will believe you. It's your word over mine and"—she pretended to sob, clutching at her cleavage—"Your honor, I was *so* scared! He was drinking and driving and I thought he was going to *kill* me!"

Undeterred, I advanced on her again, pointing at the scars on my face to try and give her a fucking reality check. "Look at what you did to me! Does that even register in your fucked-up head? *You* did this!"

"*You* were driving," she shot back, shoving me backward as if she could distance herself from the truth. "You did it to yourself, you spoiled, overgrown man-child!"

"You yanked on the wheel, you crazy bitch! You're lucky we didn't fucking die!"

"I wish you did, you miserable bastard!" She lunged forward, slamming her fists against any part of me she could reach, punctuating each word with another strike. "You cost me my job at the agency by being a selfish prick, as usual! Refusing to turn over your goddamn manuscript just to spite me! Now I have nothing and it's because of you, you fucking asshole!"

Before the accident, I could endure her attacks. Her punches and slaps hurt, but they were tolerable, in part because of my size. In my current state, with the loss of so much muscle? It was agony. Every time her rings dug into my left side or her nails raked across my skin, pain surged through my ruined body. Half the time that side was numb and refused to function the way it should, and yet when it came to pain, everything was magnified by the damaged nerves. How the hell was that fair?

Turning my face away from her flailing hands, I made a blind grab for her wrists. As soon as I got a hold of her, I pushed her away from me as hard as I could since I no longer had the strength to subdue her by force.

She stumbled backward on her heels, crashing into one of

the sofa tables. Her face contorted with outrage as she steadied herself. Before I even realized what she was going to do next, she picked up one of the porcelain figurines from the table and hurled it at me.

I barely had enough time to shield my face. The figurine bounced off my shoulder and plummeted to the parquet floor, shattering.

Another one came right behind it. Down the row she went, launching each and every one of my mother's antiques at me. Some broke against my body, others waited until they hit the floor.

"For Christ's sake, Faye!" I winced and tried to hide my face as another statuette sailed through the air. One of the sharper edges dug into my cheek, below my right eye, before smashing on the ground. Thankfully it didn't break the skin. God knows I couldn't afford to lose my one good eye to another of her outbursts. "Enough already! You've made your fucking point!"

"Fuck you, Gerulf!" Instead of taking the wind out of her sails, all my words seemed to do was infuriate her more. She'd run out of figurines, but she was by no means finished. The library had thousands of things she could throw at me and knowing her, she'd do just that until she wore herself out.

Snatching the vase off the end of the table, Faye stormed over to me and swung it as hard as she could at my head. Even though it was my weaker side, I threw my arm up, trying to block it. I shouldn't have bothered. My reaction time was too slow and my mangled arm was fucking useless. The glass shattered against my skull with the force of a sledgehammer.

"What the fuck are you doing?!" Zane shouted from the library doorway.

I blinked away the stars from my field of vision and looked up as he ran over, anger and confusion written plainly on his face. Without hesitating, he wedged himself between us like a referee breaking up two boxers. I thought he was protecting Faye from me until his arms wrapped around my torso and he forced me backward, *away* from her, making himself a barrier.

Faye lunged for me again. Before she could sink her claws in, Gilroy appeared and seized her from behind. She shrieked like a banshee and tried to free herself, but Gilroy held on, wrestling her toward the door. I was glad to see his skills were still sharp after a two-year hiatus, but horrified he had to intervene again.

"Call the police," Zane shouted at someone I couldn't see. Probably Mrs. Potter. She was never far whenever Faye was around. "And an ambulance!"

"No," I said with a shake of my head. Pain flared in my skull, making me regret the movement. "Don't call anyone."

Fury replaced the confusion on Zane's face, an emotion I didn't think was possible for someone like him. "Look at what she did to you! She needs to be arrested!"

"Just let her go." I pressed the heel of my hand against my head and sucked in a sharp breath, dropping it immediately. Blood streaked across my palm. Why did head wounds have to bleed so much? The only positive was that it was on the side that was already hideous so I wasn't at risk for any more scars —or brain damage.

Faye continued to scream at me as Gilroy forcibly removed her from the library, then the house. It was more of the same vitriol echoing off the walls: cursing my existence; wishing I was dead; hoping I'd die alone and miserable in this house; guaranteeing she'd ruin my career if it's the last thing she did.

Once upon a time, I'd confused her anger with passion. I'd forgiven her insane jealousy and her violent attacks because of how much she claimed to love me in the calm moments. In the beginning, I'd tell myself, she never *really* hurt me. She didn't *mean* to—until she did.

By the time the crocodile tears stopped falling, the criticisms were never-ending, complete with an array of smacks, slaps, and scratches to emphasize her displeasure. It had crossed the line from ardor to abuse but I was in too deep, a fact she reminded me of often. I couldn't call the police because she'd lie with the skill of an award-winning actress. Best-case scenario, they'd call us mutual combatants and leave us alone to continue our battle. The worst-case scenario would end up with me in jail and my career in ruins—something *else* she reminded me of. She held all the power in her perfectly manicured claws.

The accident had given me absolute clarity into how unbelievably cruel she was, but it was too late to do anything about it. I'd already put up with it for years—pressing charges after the fact seemed like a moot point and would *definitely* ruin my career. All I wanted now was to get her out of my life for good. Thankfully, it sounded like my wish came true and the people at Lumière Literary Agency finally got sick of her shit too.

"Come sit down," Zane said softly, taking my elbow and gesturing toward the couch.

"I'd rather go upstairs. I don't want to be here when they come clean up this mess." I cut myself off before "Again" slipped out. God knew the maids had had their fair share of cleaning up a variety of shattered materials after one of her rampages—lamps, bottles, chairs, windows, and now priceless antiques my mother had spent years collecting.

Zane nodded and steered me around the debris field. Bits of glass and porcelain crunched beneath our shoes but, for the most part, we avoided the majority of it on our way out of the library.

"What a fucking mess," I muttered to myself.

"Don't worry. Lisette is already on her way with the dustpan."

I wasn't talking about the library, but I wasn't going to correct him either. Squeezing my eyes shut, I tried to inhale slow breaths to quell the rising nausea. I was so fucking embarrassed on *so* many levels. Zane should never have witnessed any of that. The rest of the staff were well aware of her antics, but not him. I could only imagine what he thought of me now, how much I'd fallen in his esteem. Gerulf Prince, Pulitzer-prize-winning author, wealthy, educated, former triathlete—unable to withstand the assault of a woman half his size. I didn't know what was worse, his pity or his ridicule.

Guiding me up the stairs, Zane wrapped one arm securely around my waist and held onto my shirt with his other hand like I was seconds away from collapsing. I thought he'd give me a lecture as we climbed the steps, but he didn't say anything except to murmur little things, like, "I got you," and "We're almost there."

About halfway up the staircase, I realized I was leaning against him. Despite his slim build, he didn't cave under my weight. He was so much stronger than I originally gave him credit for, emotionally as well as physically. Upon first glance, I'd dismissed him, but I was man enough to admit how wrong I'd been.

I didn't have the foggiest idea how I would convince him to stay on past the end of his contract, but I needed to find a way—fast. As much as it pained me to admit, I needed his help, not just with *Loss of Twilight*, but with everything else too. I needed his support, his confidence, his kindness. I needed... *him*.

Chapter Nine

ZANE

"Don't lay down yet," I said, kneeling quickly to slide Gerulf's shoes off before he inadvertently got glass in his sheets. "And the sweater," I said as I got to my feet, holding my hand out for it.

"Not a fucking chance."

"Seriously?! You probably have glass embedded in the fabric. Plus, you're bleeding. But go ahead. Ruin your million-thread count Egyptian cotton sheets."

"They're eight hundred," he countered with a glare.

"Take your goddamn shirt off, Gerulf!" It probably wasn't the best thing in the world to be yelling at him after yet another head injury, but there was no other way to get him to listen to reason. Maybe if he wasn't so stubborn, this could have gone a lot smoother. But look who I was talking to—the King of Stubborn.

Huffing, he did as he was told. *Finally*. Wadding up the sweater, he threw it to the side and immediately crossed his arms over his chest, cementing his gaze to the floor while his jaw shifted irritably.

It wasn't a mystery why he'd wanted to keep his shirt on.

At one time, you could tell he'd been built, but much like his face, the left side of his body was also disfigured. It was more than scars, though. His left shoulder and bicep were undeniably mangled. All of the muscle had been cut away, leaving him with nothing but lumps of skin and bone down to his elbow. His torso was crisscrossed with scars—burns, surgical, and evidence of his own skin grafting. Some parts were the same color as the rest of him, but others ranged from dark red to an alarming purplish hue to stark white scar tissue. It looked painful, even now, and explained the army of pill bottles on his bedside table.

I didn't let my gaze linger in any one spot, looking just long enough to determine he wasn't bleeding from his body. "Don't move," I said, holding up a finger and darting into the master bathroom.

Rummaging around in the cabinet beneath the sink, I grabbed the stuff I thought I'd need and piled it onto a hand towel before snagging a washcloth from the linen closet. As I wet it under the faucet, waiting for the water to get warm, I stared at the wall in front of me.

The wallpaper was a patterned navy, so dark it looked black with the lighting. It wasn't what *was* there so much as what *wasn't.* He didn't have a mirror. Doing a quick mental scan of the house, it suddenly dawned on me that there weren't *any* mirrors in any of the rooms. Not in the front entryway, not in the parlor, none of the powder rooms on the first floor. The bedroom I was staying in had one in the bathroom but that was it.

The revelation made my heart hurt even more for him.

Wringing out the washcloth a bit, I scooped up my supplies and returned to Gerulf's bed, pushing the medication out of the way to set everything down on the nightstand.

Blood had ceased trickling out of his hairline, leaving

macabre trails on his skin. That was good, but smaller spots on his face glinted in the light every time he moved.

"Shit. I think there's glass in there," I said, rifling through the first aid box for some tweezers. Tipping his chin up with one hand, I angled his face away from me and went for the biggest chunk first.

He uncrossed his arms, allowing me to move closer to see what I was doing. I ended up standing between his thighs, a position I was keenly aware of, though I tried my best not to read too much into it despite his earlier... proposition? Joke?

Plucking out the piece of glass with the tweezers, I wiped it off onto a wad of gauze and kept going. Every so often, a muscle in Gerulf's cheek twitched, but he was otherwise silent throughout the whole process. I'm sure after everything he'd been through, this was a cakewalk.

"Are you really ok?" I asked quietly, removing the last shard from his forehead.

"I'm fine."

"You should still call the cops." I set the gauze and tweezers down and picked up the washcloth, wiping away the spots of blood as they bloomed on his skin.

"It's not worth it."

"She's fucking psycho, Gerulf. She could have seriously hurt you."

"She already did. That down there was just..." He sighed and shook his head. The fact he didn't want to argue was alarming. The man *lived* for arguments, for snappy comebacks, and sarcasm as thick as molasses. I'd never seen him look defeated. No wonder *Loss of Twilight* was so visceral. After what I witnessed, I had no doubt he'd been tapping into his personal experiences with Faye. It broke my heart all over again to know he'd been living with such a nightmare, as trapped and helpless as his main character.

"Did she really cause the accident?" I asked, trying to keep the emotion out of my voice.

"You were eavesdropping?" His head turned toward me, his good eye narrowed, until I pushed it back the other way so I could clean the blood out of his hair.

"When she's shouting loud enough for the whole house to hear, I wouldn't call that eavesdropping." I was totally eavesdropping. I mean, I just so happened to be standing near one of the vents down the hall that also happened to more or less echo everything being screamed in the library. I'd caught other staff members standing in that exact same spot on more than one occasion, especially when Gerulf was in a particularly foul mood, so of course that's where I headed when I left Faye and Gerulf in the library. No surprise, Mrs. Potter and Gilroy were already clustered together, their faces drawn in concern and their ears perked toward the vent.

When glass started breaking, Mrs. Potter grabbed my arm and told me not to interfere, that Gerulf would be even more pissed at *me* than that psycho in stilettos. I told her he could be as pissed as he wanted but there was no way in hell I was going to stand there and *not* do something to try and separate them.

After a stubborn moment of silence, Gerulf sighed. He practically wilted in front of me, exhaustion replacing his usual hubris. "Yeah. We were in the Alps, on our way back to the resort from dinner. Arguing. Shocking, I know. I don't even remember what had her so pissed off. I guess it doesn't matter. She started hitting me and the next thing I knew, she grabbed the fucking wheel. I threw her off, but it was too late. It was icy. I overcorrected, and we rolled. And kept rolling, right off the road and down the side of that fucking mountain.

"I took the brunt of it. I was trapped for... I don't know. It felt like forever. I was pretty much crushed on that side, which wasn't good, but then a fire started to spread. I don't remember anything after that, just pain and gagging on the smell of burning plastic. Mark said they thought I was dead when they finally pulled me out.

"I couldn't even leave Switzerland, I was in such bad shape. Mark stayed with me for a while, then he brought Mrs. Potter over. She took care of me until I could fly home a couple weeks later." He squeezed his eyes shut and swallowed thickly.

"Where was *she* at?" I didn't even want to say her name. I knew I couldn't do it without snarling like some deranged guard dog.

He chuckled and swatted my hand away from his hair so he could look up at me. "That bitch flew home the next day and practically cleared out my bank account. She told everyone it was for my treatment. So imagine my surprise when Mark told me I was fucking broke. Oh, and the engagement was off. She left me a voicemail. Whoa! Watch it!"

"Sorry." I jumped and moved the washcloth away from him, returning it to the nightstand. I hadn't even realized I was squeezing it so tightly until I spotted the drip marks on his pants.

"So that's why I have to get this book finished," he continued, letting his gaze drift away again. "The money from the advance is gone, to pay my medical expenses. If I don't deliver, they'll take me to court to get the advance back, plus money that I don't have for punitive damages. And now she's trying to fucking sue me for pain and suffering from the accident. Two years to the day, the fucking bitch."

"She can't do that!"

"It's America. She can and she did." He looked up again, his brow furrowed. "Why are you so mad?"

"Because it's bullshit! She can't do that to you, on top of everything else, and keep getting away with it!"

"It's America," he repeated slowly. "She *can* and she *did*.

No one believes a man when he says his fiancée smacks him around or when she jerked the steering wheel. They take one look at us and one look at them and decide it can't be true because women don't 'do' that, despite the statistics saying otherwise. Men are the abusers, women are the victims. Period."

"It *shouldn't* be that way."

"But it is." He put his hands on my hips and pushed me back a couple of steps so he could stand, offering no more than a dejected shrug, as if there was nothing else to say on the matter. I didn't know where he was going or what he was planning on doing once he was vertical, but my sappy little heart derailed whatever he was about to do.

Without even thinking, I took a step closer and wrapped my arms around his neck, hugging him as tightly as I dared. I mean, the line between personal and professional was already blurry, so who cared if this obliterated whatever was left? He needed a fucking hug after the night he was having and I needed him to know that I believed him.

For months I'd smelled traces of his cologne whenever we were near each other, a dark spiciness that suited his wealth and attitude perfectly. Up close, like this, I got the unfiltered version and I reveled in it. His scent, the warmth of his skin—it all stoked feelings inside of me I should *not* have for any straight guy, let alone my boss, but I couldn't help myself when it came to him.

Predictably, Gerulf tensed against me. "What are you doing?"

"You seem like you could use a hug," I answered truthfully.

"I'm not—I don't—I don't *hug*, Zane. People don't—"

"Just accept the hug, Gerulf."

He cleared his throat, but at least he quit arguing. For all his flirting or teasing or whatever it was earlier, he sure did clam up when actually presented with human contact. I couldn't help but wonder how long it had been since anyone *had* hugged him. Or simply touched him beyond what was routine in his numerous medical appointments.

I don't know how long we stayed like that, me holding him and him barely even breathing as he stood there, arms hanging straight at his sides. Awkwardness and self-doubt crept in with each passing second until I was thoroughly convinced Gerulf would fire me as soon as he got over the shock of forced affection. I decided all of his earlier teasing had been just that. Teasing. Trying to get a rise out of me since he'd backed off a bit from his usual level of biting sarcasm, trading it for something more playful. And I was an idiot to think it was something, anything, else. Something more.

Forcing myself to pull away, I was surprised when I didn't get far.

Gerulf's hands touched my waist, so lightly I almost thought I was imagining it. Gradually, his hands moved further, until his arms were entirely around my waist and our bodies were pressed together in a proper embrace.

I tried to squash the feelings inside and cram them back into the fantasy box they belonged in, but the longer we held each other, the more they came rushing out. When his lips grazed the side of my neck, the truth hit me like a freight train.

This wasn't just a crush I'd been harboring. I loved him.

I didn't want to.

I didn't plan to.

And yet, I did.

I loved his brashness, his scathing sarcasm, his brilliant mind. I loved his pride, his independence, and the way he was when it was just the two of us, when he could actually let his guard down. I loved the way he listened to me, the way he *saw* me, and how he immortalized my best traits on paper for the world to read. He made me feel like I mattered as a whole person, instead of being reduced to a single aspect like a brain or a pretty face.

I loved him for all of that and so much more. And I think, by the way he was slowly nuzzling my neck, he might have been hinting at his own feelings earlier, before we were rudely interrupted.

Our chests rose and fell in tandem, like puzzle pieces slotting together. "Gerulf..."

He turned toward me, caressing the side of my face. "Yes?"

"I need you to fire me," I whispered.

A small crease formed between his dark eyebrows. "Why?"

"So I can kiss you without feeling guilty."

"Zane." He cleared his throat softly and my heart seized, refusing to start again until he spoke. "You're fired."

The words had barely left his lips when mine crashed against his. He threaded his fingers through my hair and angled my head for a deeper kiss, sweeping his velvety tongue over mine. I melted against him, not caring if this was right or wrong or how it would ultimately end. All I cared about was the man right in front of me and making Gerulf see how incredible he was, that he wasn't the monster Faye made him out to be. Most importantly, I wanted him to feel loved, even if it was only for one night.

Chapter Ten

GERULF

The feeling of Zane's arms around me unleashed a torrent of emotions, so much so that I stood there like an idiot for what seemed like forever, trying to make sense of them all. How long *had* it been since anyone hugged me? I shuddered to think Faye was the last person, but it had to have been her. For the past two years, the only people who had any reason to touch me were doctors or nurses and they certainly weren't hugging me. I could barely even get a handshake from most people. I forgot how warm and solid another person could feel. How good they could smell. Like mint and citrus. Clean and calming.

As I was processing the different sensations, Zane's muscles went rigid, preparing to spring away. I couldn't let that happen, not while I was still marveling at his closeness. Every fiber of my being screamed at me to stop him so I could keep soaking up his warmth like a sponge, but if he really wanted to leave I knew I couldn't force him to stay.

That didn't mean I couldn't give him a signal, something small to let him know I was receptive to his hug in spite of my initial shock. If he'd had a change of heart, the gesture could easily be explained away, like our earlier banter in the library.

Holding my breath, I lifted my hands to his slim waist, encircling it slowly, hoping it was enough to get him to pause and reconsider leaving.

Like a deer sensing a change on the wind, Zane froze in place, still within the circle of my arms. Heartened that he stayed, I pulled him back in for a real hug, this time with my arms around him. His dark curls brushed against my cheek, beckoning me closer. My lips grazed along the pulse point fluttering in the side of his neck. As much as I wanted to kiss his beautiful mouth, I'd happily settle for the soft skin along his throat. Everything about him was soft. And gentle. But none of that was to say he was weak. After all, he'd stood his ground against me for months without caving.

Zane's breath quickened before he spoke. "Gerulf..."

My heart clenched at the way he said my name. Was this it? Was this the part where he ran away? I forced myself to look at him, to accept the rejection that was coming. But even still, I couldn't stop from touching his face, letting my thumb sweep across the pinkness in his smooth cheek. "Yes?"

"I need you to fire me." He may have whispered the words, but the look in his dark eyes was serious.

"Why?"

"So I can kiss you without feeling guilty."

"Zane." I cleared my throat, trying to get the words to come out. Even though it's what I wanted from Day One, and it's what he wanted now, I dreaded having to say them. "You're fired."

Zane rushed forward, slanting his lips over mine. I slid my hand into his hair, cupping the back of his head while my mouth ravaged his. His lips, his tongue, all soft and silken and just the way I'd imagined. He moaned into our kiss, pressing himself against me to get as close as he could, a notion that still amazed me.

Even more amazing was the fact his cock hardened as we kissed. Our lengths rubbed against one another with each shift and swivel of our hips, but I was desperate for more. I slid one arm around his waist and grabbed his ass, yanking his hips forward for more friction for both of us. Running his hands down my chest, down my stomach, he wedged one hand between us, groping the bulge in my pants.

"I want you Gerulf. I want to feel you. *All* of you," he murmured between kisses, stroking my cock through the fabric.

"I want that too."

"But?"

"I... I haven't been with—I haven't done this in a while." Since he hadn't slowed his hand at all, I practically panted the words, hoping to God they didn't make him stop. A while? What the hell was a "while," anyway? It had been almost two decades since college and I hadn't known what I was doing then, either. Alcohol had helped but I didn't have that luxury this time around. It felt like my first time all over again. The nerves were worse, actually, since I had the physical *and* psychological impact of my scars to contend with this time, *plus* the sobriety.

Instead of bolting for the door, a soft smile curved his lips before he kissed me. He abandoned my cock to run his hands through my hair, holding me in place as he kissed me slowly, resetting the pace. And I let him. Whether it was a sudden burst of shyness on my part, or insecurity, or whatever—I let Zane take the lead, knowing I could trust him to be gentle.

As if he could read my thoughts, he nudged me toward the bed. We slid in that direction until the back of my thighs hit the mattress.

"Lay down," he said.

I climbed into bed and scooted backward, giving him room to do whatever it was he had planned.

He tugged his shirt over his head and tossed it to the side before following me. Instead of going straight for my pants, he crawled up onto my lap and straddled me carefully, running his fingertips over my bare chest. He didn't seem to pay any particular attention to my scars, nor did he avoid them entirely. He touched me, everywhere, without flinching or gagging, without any outward expression at all except perhaps a combination of curiosity and awe.

"Is this ok?" he asked as he skimmed his hands over my body, gradually adding a bit more pressure to the left side.

I nodded, pulling his torso down on top of mine. Brushing his dark curls out of my way so I could kiss his neck, I nipped now and again on my way to his earlobe. He tipped his head back with a sigh, giving me greater access to his throat. At the same time, he threaded his fingers into my hair and down to the base of my skull, keeping my mouth close to his skin until he turned toward me and captured my lips with his.

It was my turn to sigh into that kiss, his lush lips and soft tongue moving perfectly with mine. Kissing him was what epic stories were made of, what kisses were meant to be. I could spend hours kissing him and never grow tired of it. When he pulled his mouth away, I actually growled in frustration.

"You're not in charge anymore, Mr. Prince," Zane said, swiveling his hips, purposely rubbing his cock against mine with a devilish smirk. "So huffing and puffing isn't going to get you what you want."

"No? Then what will?" I grabbed his hips and ground myself against him, trying to find some relief for my aching dick now that it had been awakened from its hibernation period.

"Use that big vocabulary of yours and ask." He pinched my nipple to emphasize his point, his dark eyes molten as he gazed down at me. That look alone had my cock straining in my pants, growing more and more desperate for freedom as it slid against his ass.

"I just want you," I said, feeling more than a twinge of vulnerability at the confession.

"You have me," he whispered, leaning down and pressing his lips to mine. I ran my hands over his ass and up his smooth back, tangling them in his messy curls again. He flicked his tongue over my lips as he pulled away. "I'll be right back."

"Where are you going?"

"You'll see." He slipped off my lap slowly and stood, as languid as a cat, a coy smile on his face.

Brow furrowed, I propped myself up on my elbows, watching him pad back to the bathroom.

A moment later, he returned with a bottle of body oil and a towel.

"Found this too," he said, holding up a condom before tossing it on the nightstand next to the oil. "If you want to, I mean."

Was that a trick question? I wasn't sure, so I didn't say anything.

Either Zane didn't notice or he wasn't put off by my silence. He simply removed his pants and returned to the bed, his underwear still in place as he tugged my pants off as well.

"Roll over," he said.

"I don't really like massages," I bit out, still hung up on the fact he sought out a condom, but also by the fact he wanted to touch me beyond what was required for him to get off. "The nurse does it. They don't feel good."

"I'm not the nurse." Zane smiled softly and poured a small bit of oil into his palm, making a show of rubbing his hands together. Once it was warmed up, he wrapped his hands around my foot and used his thumbs to massage small circles on the ball of my foot.

I stiffened for a moment until the foreign sensation faded to one of pleasure, even relaxation.

"I've been with you for almost six months," Zane said, working the arch of my foot with a calm determination to prove his point, "and I've never seen you relax."

"I don't know how," I replied, letting my lids drift shut.

He laughed softly. "Clearly."

"I see your sympathy only goes so far."

"About as far as your patience."

I cracked an eye to glare at him but was met with a beatific smile. Shaking my head, I forced myself to exhale a slow breath. Instead of worrying about what he was thinking or trying to scrutinize every look on his face, I focused on how good his hands felt as they worked along my body methodically, moving from my feet and up my legs, inch by inch.

When he got to my thighs, my dick twitched in anticipation, my hard-on reviving from his proximity. It was standing at full attention by the time he got done slathering more oil on his palms.

Sadly, his hands swept right past my groin and up my abdomen to my chest. He started with my non-scarred side, massaging my shoulder and along the length of my arm to my hand, lavishing as much attention on each individual finger as he had every other part of me. If he was this attentive before sex had even begun, I was dying to know what he'd be like in the midst of it.

If he wanted to, that is. I mean, he must have. He went looking for a condom and found it. It's not like I kept them front and center in the cabinet, so he'd had to sift through the bathroom drawers, which spoke to his objective.

The real question was—could I even get there? Sex hadn't been a factor in my life since well before the accident and it certainly wasn't a priority afterward. Physical hideousness and emotional unavailability aside, there was the medical aspect to consider. It was a miracle I'd been able to maintain a hard-on this long. Would it last? If it did, would I even manage to reach a climax?

Time was suddenly of the essence. Fear of failure and humiliation loomed on the horizon. If I didn't take advantage of the situation now, while I was at full mast, I ran the risk of leaving Zane wholly unsatisfied. After everything he'd done for me, that was the *last* thing I wanted to do.

"Take these off," I said, slipping my hand beneath the waistband of his underwear and running my palm over the curve of his ass.

A slow smile tugged the corner of his mouth as he climbed off the bed again. He did as he was told, shedding them without fanfare.

I shifted back into the pillows into somewhat of a sitting position and peeled my own off, tossing them to the floor as he resumed his position above me.

"My God, you're beautiful." The words were out before I could stop myself. I didn't know if he'd be offended by that historically effeminate word, but it was the only one that came to mind when I looked at him. Beautiful hair, beautiful eyes, beautiful skin, beautiful smile. More importantly, he had a beautiful soul, as banal as *that* sounded. He was just one of those genuinely good people in the world; he needed to be protected at all costs and cherished daily by someone who knew how extraordinary he was. Someone like me.

The blush I loved stained his cheeks immediately. He tried to hide it by ducking his head and turning his attention to my cock, but I saw it all the same. My chest squeezed, knowing that somehow, even after our tumultuous beginning, I'd managed to win the affection of someone like him. Someone good and kind-hearted who wasn't chasing after my looks or money or influence. Someone who wanted *me*, massive flaws and all.

"Should I get the condom for this part?" he asked as he shifted to the side, kneeling next to me so he could stroke my cock with the same unhurried movements he'd used during my massage.

"Only if you want to."

Apparently, he didn't want to, since the next thing I knew, the hot, wet perfection of his mouth wrapped around my dick and slid down my shaft.

I gasped like a goddamn moron. Touching me was one thing, but his mouth? Fuck. I guess I didn't need to worry about any side effects from the medication because I was ready to climax right then and there.

In spite of how good it felt, I couldn't just lay there and enjoy it. I wanted the pleasure to be mutual. Snagging the bottle of oil, I dripped some on his glorious ass and massaged it into his cheeks. With each pass, my hand drifted closer and closer to the center until my pinky grazed his taint. He didn't object, nor did he flinch when I slipped my finger along his crease, skimming over his hole and circling the rim.

Instead, he moaned around my dick and angled himself toward me to make his ass easier to reach. Squirting some more oil on my hand, I rubbed it between his cheeks, making sure there was plenty there before I started teasing his hole in earnest, alternating between light strokes and rubbing somewhat harder circles to help stretch the area.

"Is this ok?" I asked, a strange reversal of our earlier conversation.

"Yeah," he breathed, flicking his tongue over my slit as his slippery palm slid up and down my shaft.

"Can I go farther?"

"Just go slow."

Permission granted, I pressed one finger inside, easing it in from knuckle to knuckle between his gasps and sighs, until it was all the way in. I let it sit for a moment in the tight heat of his body before gradually moving my finger in and out, exploring each new sensation and committing it to memory, along with whatever reaction I garnered from Zane. One spot, in particular, got him to clench around me with a satisfied groan and I immediately put it at the top of my list of things to repeat.

"Oh, fuck. Right there," he moaned, grinding against my hand and stroking my cock faster.

Slicking my hand with extra oil, I worked two fingers inside his hole, concentrating on the spot that made goosebumps spread over his pale skin.

"Oh my God. Yes." He bucked back against my hand a couple of times before leaning down and swallowing my cock whole, sucking and licking and stroking it with abandon.

I squeezed my eyes shut, trying to stave off the waves of pleasure racing through me. I knew it had been a while, but damn… It was easily the best blowjob of my life. And the more I fucked him with my fingers, the more zealously he sucked and stroked my cock.

On the verge of coming in his amazing mouth, I blurted out, "Get the condom." Biting my lip, I forced myself to think of anything I could to keep from climaxing, letting a stream of decidedly un-sexy images run rampant in my brain.

"Are you ok?"

"I don't know how much longer I'm going to last."

He gave me an impish grin as he leaned over me to grab the condom from the nightstand. "You don't need to rush anything. We've got the whole night, you know."

"Maybe *you* do, but I sure as hell don't. It's a miracle we've even gotten this far."

His dark eyes softened. "Are you really ok? You're not in pain or anything?"

"I'm fine," I replied with a small smile, caressing his face in an attempt to assuage his visible worry. "I want to make sure you cross the finish line, that's all."

He leaned into my touch, his cheeks flushing again. "That's not what sex is supposed to be about. I mean, it's nice, but I care more about this right here than some 'finish line.'"

"You continue to mystify me, Zane Beaumont." I studied his face for the millionth time, from the way his dark lashes framed his guileless eyes to the shy smile on his kiss-swollen lips.

"Does that mean you want to stop?"

"Absolutely not." I took the condom from him and tore it open, rolling it on as quickly as I could.

Once it was in place, Zane straddled my lap again. I let him hold my cock steady, positioning it where it needed to be as he sank onto it slowly, swiveling his hips now and again to help it along. He took it all the way to the hilt with a gasp, swearing softly under his breath as his ass came flush with my pelvis.

"Oh, fuck." My head thunked against the headboard, overwhelmed by the constricting heat surrounding my cock and the fact this was really happening.

"Does that feel ok?"

"It's perfect. You're perfect. Are you ok?"

Grabbing my face between his hands, Zane kissed me hotly, swirling his tongue with mine. We stayed like that for a while, kissing each other as if our lives depended on it. Once he'd acclimated, Zane began to rock his hips, studying me as intently as I was studying him, each of us apparently on the lookout for any sign of discomfort. I ran my hands up and down his body as he moved on top of me, caressing his thighs and hips and chest. When it became clear neither of us was in any sort of pain, he bounced a little harder, a little faster, gripping the headboard for balance as he rode me, his dick bobbing in front of him.

As good as he felt, I wanted more. The animalistic part of me needed more. I didn't just want to have sex, I wanted to fuck him, to dominate him, to give him pleasure instead of merely being a means for him to give it to himself.

"Let's stand," I said.

Zane nodded and carefully slid off. "Where?"

"Here is fine." I cupped the back of his neck and yanked him forward, kissing him hard. He responded in kind, his fingers groping and clawing my chest and shoulders, trying to pull me closer. I spun him away from me, kissing the curve of his neck and along his shoulder before I bent him over the edge of the bed.

I was going to make sure this position was alright with him but before I could double-check, he spread his stance and arched his back, which I took to mean he was on board with the plan.

Gripping his asscheek in one hand, I eased my cock inside of him with the other, sliding in slow and deep to draw out Zane's beautiful moan. He rose up on the tips of his toes before forcing himself back down, pushing back against me. I withdrew my cock as slowly as I entered, thrusting back in a little faster. In and out, slow and then fast and slow again. I tried to make it feel good for him in addition to lasting as long as I could. From the way he panted into the mattress and clutched the sheets, I had a feeling I was doing something right.

"Fuck, Gerulf!"

Wrapping my hand around his messy curls, I tugged his head back, lowering my mouth to his ear. "You like it like this?"

He couldn't nod with my hand in his hair, but he managed to moan out, "Uh huh."

"You want more?"

"Uh huh."

Releasing his hair, I gathered his wrists and stacked them on top of each other, pinning them to the small of his back with one hand. Spitting into my palm, I reached around to his cock with the other, stroking it as best I could while I drove into him. My hips snapped against his perfect ass, again and again, as the pleasure inside of me swelled.

"Oh my God, I'm gonna come," Zane panted, his nails digging into his own wrists as he held onto himself. "Don't stop. Don't fucking stop." Muffling his cry into the bedding, he clenched around my cock as his own erupted, shooting cum like a volcano all over my hand.

"Fuck!" I pumped into him a couple more times before I spilled my release with a groan, nearly collapsing on top of him from the sheer exhaustion of it all. Every muscle in my body would hate me in the morning, but I didn't care. It was worth it. *Zane* was worth it. Besides, I'd take this over regular physical therapy any day.

Once my cock finished pulsing, I exhaled a steadying breath and released Zane's wrists, caressing his hips. He slid his arms forward, more or less propping himself up, but he made no move to stand.

Easing my cock out of him carefully, I slid the condom loose and tied it off, tossing it in the trash can by the bed.

"Are you ok?" I asked, running my hand up and down his spine. He still hadn't moved from his bent-over position, sounding alarm bells in the back of my head. I hadn't hurt him, had I? I didn't think I did and I certainly didn't mean to. We'd started slow and I wasn't exactly in peak physical condition, but it was so much easier to hurt a man than a woman. Fuck! I'd let myself get too carried away and he was too nice to say anything.

Zane barely answered with an unhelpful, "Mhmm."

I brushed his dark curls away from his face, hoping to reassure myself he wasn't lying. Opening one dark eye, he gave me a small, dreamy sort of smile to go along with the sexy flush to his pale skin. Any earlier concern melted at the sight of him, replaced with relief and pride that I was able to please him so well.

"Are *you* ok?" he asked, pushing himself up onto his elbows and tilting his head, the look of contentment still firmly in place.

"More than ok."

"Good. I'm happy to hear it." He crawled up onto the bed again and slipped beneath the comforter, making himself comfortable in the mountain of pillows next to my usual spot.

Since I didn't know what the post-sex protocol was supposed to be in this day and age, I decided to lay next to him and let him call the shots again. If he wanted a shower, we'd shower. If he wanted to leave, I wouldn't stop him. And if he wanted to stay? A large part of me hoped he would simply because I wasn't ready to say goodbye to him in *any* capacity, even if it was only to say goodnight.

I was way too hot and sweaty to actually want to cuddle, but I smiled to myself when Zane rolled over to face me and laced our fingers together. Holding someone's hand shouldn't have made my heart skip a beat, especially not after we'd already had sex, but it did. I didn't know if it was because I'd wanted to hold his hand for so long, or if it was because he was willingly touching me again, even with post-orgasm clarity. Either way, I didn't care so long as he didn't let go.

"Was it everything you remembered?" Zane asked, biting his lower lip to try and hide a mischievous smirk.

"Uh, no. It was better. Way better."

"Well good. I'm glad."

"Was it ok for you?"

"More than ok," he quipped with a bright smile.

"You know, you look all nice and innocent, but you've got

quite the sarcastic streak underneath that doe-eyed persona of yours."

His smile broadened. "Maybe you're rubbing off on me."

"I don't know if that's a good thing or not."

"Time will tell." He leaned forward, kissing me gently.

Chapter Eleven

GERULF

The next morning, I woke up to something I never thought I'd see—Zane, asleep in my bed. If I wasn't looking at him, if I couldn't feel his skin against mine, I would have thought I was dreaming. On paper, there was no way someone like Zane should ever want to be with someone like me. Yet there he was, wrapped up in my sheets with his arm draped over my chest.

As the minutes passed, my initial happiness faded until only fear remained.

What would he say when he woke up?

What would he *do* when he woke up?

Would he leave? Was he serious about that whole firing thing or was it supposed to be symbolic?

Was this a one-time thing? A novel way to usher in a new year? Or worse—was it a pity lay? A parting gift, a mercy, before he went and lived out the rest of his life with someone who wasn't an irascible son of a bitch.

I thought he enjoyed it. He *seemed* to enjoy it. The end result told me he enjoyed it. What if it was all for show? Guys could and did fake orgasms, but he hadn't faked ejaculating all over my hand. Oh, God! What if he was doing this for blackmail? He knew about Faye, though. And he was smart enough to know you couldn't squeeze blood out of a turnip. Unless he was counting on my future royalties like that bitch was with her bullshit lawsuit.

I nearly jumped out of my skin when Zane's hand slid over my chest and up to my face, his fingers splaying along the stubble on my cheek.

"You know you look angry, even while you're asleep?" Zane murmured as he shifted closer, burying his face in the side of my neck and peppering my skin with soft kisses.

"Now, how would I know that?"

"God, you're grumpy in the morning." It didn't deter him from pressing himself along the length of me or from sliding his long leg over mine, wriggling as close as humanly possible.

The central question in my brain came out in a rush. "Did you mean it last night? Or was it just..." A mistake? A game? Boredom? Charity? I couldn't even say the words. *Any* words. Mainly because I was afraid if I said them out loud and he said yes, I'd feel like an even bigger idiot than I did already for thinking this tryst would turn into something it never could.

"Hey..." Zane propped himself up on an elbow and caressed the side of my face. His fingertips ended up tracing the jagged scars in my skin, but I couldn't tell if it was on purpose or because of how fucking big and hideous they were, making them hard to miss. "What's the matter?"

I pushed his arm out of the way and sat up, throwing the covers back, but he didn't let me out of bed. He grabbed onto my bicep—the one that *wasn't* mangled—and used it to drag himself forward so he was right behind me.

"Gerulf, wait. I'm sorry for making that crack about you looking angry. It was just the way your jaw was set. I didn't mean anything by it."

"It's not that."

"Ok. Did I do something? Or say something else that was wrong?"

"No. Of course not."

"Then talk to me."

"Things are different in daylight. *People* are different. The choice you made last night—"

"Last night was perfect," he said softly, reaching for my face. I yielded under his touch, allowing him to turn me so he could meet my gaze. "Don't second-guess it because the sun is up. And please don't push me away. Not now."

"How can you stand to touch me? To see me? Like *this*?"

"Like what?" His dark brows dipped as he ran his thumb along one of the scars on my face. When he reached the end, he let his hand drift to my gnarled shoulder and down what was left of my arm, back over to my torso and the hideous assortment of discolored skin and scars. "I see *you*, Gerulf. I don't know who you were before and I don't care. *This* is the version of you I fell in love with." He squeezed his eyes shut and swore under his breath, retracting his hand. "I'm sorry. I didn't—that wasn't—what I *meant* to say was—"

As soon as I processed his exact words, I caught his face between my hands. Pulling him closer, I pressed my lips against his, silencing whatever ridiculous apology he was going to try and make for *my* insecurities and putting an end to whatever nonsensical doubts lingered for either one of us.

In the wake of his confession, pieces of my heart unfurled themselves, pieces I thought had shriveled up and died years ago. Turned out they were simply dormant, waiting for the warmth of a long overdue spring.

Never breaking the kiss, Zane shifted forward into my lap and nudged me to lie down. Once I was reclined beneath him, his lips trailed off to the left side of my face, kissing my scars gently and with zero hesitation.

Caressing his jaw, I turned him toward me again so I could

marvel at the sight of him in daylight. His pale skin contrasted with the flush in his cheeks and the darkness of his long, curly hair. It was his eyes I focused on, though, a dark brown so warm and truthful in a world of artifice. And when he smiled? Soft and knowing, full of a quiet confidence I'd leaned on more than once over the past few months. How could this be anything *but* love? For both of us.

"I love you too," I said, in answer to the unspoken question that flashed across his face. "And I want you to stay. Here. With me. Don't leave when your contract is up."

His smile brightened as he leaned down, kissing me until we were both breathless.

IT WAS MID-MORNING BY THE TIME I MANAGED TO stumble down the stairs to what was surely a cold breakfast. I didn't care. For the first time in *years,* I could say I was happy. I'd choke down rubbery eggs and drink cold coffee for the rest of my life if I got to experience this feeling every day.

Mrs. Potter appeared in the hallway as soon as I hit the bottom step. Wringing her hands together, she looked like she was on the verge of tears. "Sir, there's a problem, and I didn't want to bother you with it, but I don't know what else to do."

My happiness evaporated in an instant. "What's wrong?"

"It's Mr. Beaumont. He's... he's gone!"

I blinked, my brow furrowing. "What do you mean—"

"Gone!" she repeated, practically shouting the word. "He always comes down for breakfast promptly at 7:30. Without fail. Even on the weekends. Even after his father passed. Chef has it timed perfectly. So today, when he didn't come down, Gilroy went to his room to make sure he was alright, and he's gone! His car is here, but the bed hasn't been slept in. There's no trace of him anywhere!"

"No trace of who?" Zane asked, materializing at my side, his damp hair smelling like my shampoo. "What's going on?"

"Mr. Beaumont!" Mrs. Potter threw her arms around his waist and hugged him tightly. "We thought you'd left! We thought something happened!" After a moment, she shoved him away with a scowl, all concern for his welfare gone in the blink of an eye. "Where have you been? We have searched this whole house up and down for you! *And* the gardens, despite the foot of snow out there!"

"I, um..." He shifted awkwardly next to me, flushing. "I was, um..."

"With me," I finished. To solidify my point, I laced my fingers through Zane's and waited for Mrs. Potter to put two and two together.

"With you? But—" Her confusion was immediately replaced with a delighted shriek as she squeezed an arm around both of our waists. "I'm so happy! Oh, we need to celebrate! Forget everything else in the dining room. We need something special for today." She whirled away from us, hurrying down the hallway, yelling for Gilroy and the cook to get the champagne.

"You realize she's going to tell the whole house, right?" Zane asked with a laugh.

"I have a feeling they've already been talking about it. They're not as sly as they think they are." I tugged him forward and slipped my other arm around his waist, pulling him up against me.

"Yeah, no. That kitchen is straight out of Downton Abbey with all the gossip flying around. I had the scoop on everyone within my first week."

"Then let's give them something to really talk about." I

grinned, pressing my lips to his and threading one hand through his hair.

Kissing me in spite of a smile, Zane twined his arms around my neck, molding his body to mine.

Down the hall, a door opened. There was a small gasp and a giggle, and the door closed again. Lisette, if I had to guess.

We broke apart with a laugh of our own.

Zane reclaimed my hand and we set off for the dining room at an easy stroll. "Are we going to finish your manuscript today?"

"No."

"No?"

"No. I fired you, remember?" I shot him a glance out of the corner of my eye, smirking.

"It's daytime now. You can rehire me."

"Only to fire you again when the sun goes down?"

"Yeah. Exactly."

"I appreciate your attempt at professionalism, but that ship has long since sailed."

"Meaning?"

"You're fired and you're staying fired," I said, making sure there was zero trace of humor in my tone.

A scowl crossed his face. "Gerulf."

"I'm serious. Do you know what a sexual harassment lawsuit would do to me? I can't afford to get caught having sex with my assistant, violating God only knows how many labor laws. Literally. Cannot afford it. You should see the bank statements." I finally cracked a smile to let him know I was kidding.

Zane scoffed and rolled his eyes. "I hope you have a good severance package, then."

"You didn't complain about my package last night."

"Oh my God!" His blush was damn near instantaneous and I loved it. "You're getting a one-star review on Indeed, Mr. Prince. Good luck finding another assistant."

"Ouch! One star? I thought I'd get a"—I scrunched up my face in a parody of thought—"three... at least?"

"Author is an asshole," Zane continued, folding his arms over his chest with his eyebrows raised pointedly. "Do *not* recommend working for him no matter how charming you think he is."

"Well, I guess you can kiss your reference letter goodbye, Mr. Beaumont."

"I'd like to kiss something else, if you don't mind." Laughing, he grabbed the front of my shirt and pulled me in, sealing his mouth to mine in a kiss bound to make the staff buzz even more if they saw us.

Epilogue

ZANE

Six months later

As soon as the delivery truck rumbled away from the front step, I was out the door in a flash. I snatched the package off the ground and tore into the cardboard on my way back inside, kicking the door shut behind me.

It took everything in me not to completely open the package. But this was Gerulf's book baby. It was only right *he* was the one who got to see it first, in all its physical gloriousness.

"The proof for *Twilight* is here," I said as I walked into the library. Seated on one of the antique couches next to the unlit fireplace with his chin propped on his hand, Gerulf stared at nothing. I eased onto the cushion next to him, frowning. "Are you ok?"

He blinked himself out of his reverie and nodded. "Mhmm. Did you open it?"

"No. I mean, I opened the box for you, but I didn't take it out." I held the package out to him, but he pushed it back toward me.

"You do it."

"It's *your* book."

He leveled an unimpressed look in my direction until I sighed and set the box in my lap so I could unfold the cardboard flaps. Pulling out the brown packing paper, I fished the book out of the depth of the box and turned it over.

Gleaming up at me on the front cover of a hefty six-by-nine hardcover was my name. *My* name. On a real book.

The title was sandwiched between *both* of our names. In the same font. Same size. Same central location. As a co-author. Gerulf Prince *and* Zane Beaumont.

"Gerulf..." I didn't even know what I wanted to say. All I could do was stare at the precious gift in my hands, at a loss for actual words.

"This book wouldn't have happened without you," Gerulf said, squeezing my thigh gently. "You saved my career, Zane. Hell, we both know you did more than that. If it wasn't for you, I would have never made it. Not with the book, or the lawsuit..." He swallowed thickly, but his voice remained raspy. "You saved me. This was the only thing I could do to show the world how special you are, to even try and repay you for everything you've given me."

A swirl of emotions radiated through me—happiness, shock, love, more shock. I threw my arms around his neck, hugging him tightly before claiming his lips in a kiss I hoped conveyed all of those feelings, along with my gratitude.

After spending every day with this man for almost a year, he still found ways to surprise me. First, as my cantankerous employer, who wanted absolutely nothing to do with me until one random day he didn't look at me with contempt anymore. Over time, our relationship blossomed into something... more. Calling him my boyfriend wasn't enough to encapsulate everything he meant to me. And now he'd gone and done this—submitted the manuscript to his publisher and, without my knowledge, included me as a co-author even though he didn't have to. I would have been happy to see my name in the acknowledgments. But to be on the front cover? I almost pinched myself.

It was kind of like the day Faye's lawyers withdrew her frivolous lawsuit and then distanced themselves from her as quickly as they could. After Mr. Abner answered the complaint on Gerulf's behalf, unequivocally naming Faye as the negligent party in the accident, the lengthy discovery process began. It was a battle fought outside the courtroom before any sort of trial, using a plethora of legal terms and posturing in the hopes of pressuring the other side to agree to a settlement, in her case, or give up, in Gerulf's.

During depositions of every single person on Gerulf's staff, her side realized they had a big fucking problem—Faye herself.

It turned out Mrs. Potter and Gilroy *hadn't* been ignoring what was happening in the mansion. Like always, they just didn't tell Gerulf about what they were up to. When Faye's lawyers sat them down, they pulled out piles of evidence damning their client—records, going back years, documenting the abuse. Dates and times had been logged meticulously in a notebook, complete with an account of who was present in the house. Photographs were taken of rooms she'd destroyed and injuries she'd inflicted on Gerulf. Audio recordings were made of her screaming at him, berating him up one side and down the other. Itzel even managed to film her outburst the night she served him with the summons, showing Gilroy dragging Faye out of the house while she promised to ruin Gerulf and take the rest of his money.

As if *that* wasn't enough, Gerulf's lawyers produced two witnesses to the accident overseas. Unfortunately for her and her sob story, the couple in the vehicle behind them saw the whole thing. They watched Faye lunge across the car before it jerked back and forth across the road as an obvious fight ensued. Helpless, they then stared in horror as the BMW careened through the guardrail and off the side of the mountain.

I had no doubt they were the only reason Gerulf was still alive because they were also the first ones to call emergency services. Two years ago, Mr. Abner had made a point to get their statements and contact information, saving it for a rainy day such as this. He'd been clued in on Faye's violent streak by Lisette during their secret courtship, something they'd hidden from the rest of the staff. Ultimately, it came to light, along with all of the other dirty little secrets in Gerulf's house.

With the deck utterly stacked against them, Faye's lawyers did the smart thing and retreated from a losing battle. A few days later, they withdrew the complaint.

As the final coup de grace, Mr. Abner provided her with a copy of her very own Non-Disclosure Agreement, the one she'd signed at the beginning of her relationship with Gerulf. If she so much as breathed Gerulf's name again, he'd make sure she was charged with violating it—in addition to Aggravated Domestic Battery, which came with mandatory imprisonment. After all, he reminded her, the statute of limitations for her case had run out… but Gerulf's hadn't.

In the days following the depositions, the staff tiptoed around Gerulf, waiting for him to unleash his wrath. He didn't. As Gilroy once said, in that house, the ends justified the means, and at the very least, they showed there wasn't anything they wouldn't do for their boss. I think Gerulf knew that, which is why he broke down when Mrs. Potter was the first to bravely march up to him and hug him, telling him how much she loved him.

Despite his initial embarrassment at finding out what they'd been doing under his very nose, there was no doubt he was grateful. The curse of Faye had been lifted at last and the whole house heaved a sigh of relief, turning their attention to a brighter future.

When I took this job last summer, I thought I knew what I was getting into. I had *no* idea. Pulling back the curtain on one of my favorite authors' lives showed me how deceptive appearances really were, even in our modern age. The man pictured on the back of those books looked like he had it all, while in reality, every day was a nightmare.

Thankfully, he didn't have to worry about any of that with me. I loved him just as he was, grumpy stubbornness and all, even if I did call him on his attitude now and again. But I wouldn't trade any of it, not our rocky beginning when I was sure he hated me (he still refuses to answer the question) or the fact his love language is snark and sarcasm, while mine is of a gentler variety. What matters is that we bring out the best in each other.

Not all fairytales start with "Once upon a time," but they all end with the same thing—*they lived happily ever after.*

And so would we.

The End

Afterword

It may seem strange to pair a wholesome tale like *Beauty and the Beast* with something as awful as domestic violence… and yet, here we are.

Advocating for men's issues has become a pillar of my brand and I won't apologize for it. That's *not* to say that every book is going to carry an overarching moral lesson, but if the opportunity presents itself to shed light on very real matters affecting the male community, then I'm going to make the most of it.

One such issue, clearly, is domestic violence and how it affects men. I could have easily made *Wither* a full-length novel full of flashbacks and drawn out the legal battle at the end to further showcase what Gerulf experienced, but I didn't think it was necessary. This was a love story, after all. I wanted it to end happily. Until this part…

But of course, whenever someone asserts that men can *absolutely* be victims of domestic violence, it seems to draw a line in the sand. I can already hear the critics gearing up. *Misogynist. Anti-feminist. Pick Me.* To which, I can only say,

"I'm not." I hope the women in this story came across as diverse as they are in real life, both good *and* bad.

In case you need further convincing, allow me to break down the roles of the female characters I "vilified" in this story. Perhaps when you see them compared to the characters we know from the very famous animators in a magical kingdom, it'll become clear why they were the way they were and misogyny had nothing to do with it.

- Oksana = Gaston; clueless, obsessive, mean-spirited, vain, utterly self-centered.
- Faye = the fairy who cursed the Beast.

And for anyone who was wondering, the "good" females actually outnumber the "bad"—Mrs. Nesbitt, Esther, Mrs. Potter, Lisette, and Itzel. Together, they showed a variety of strength, cunning, love, and humor and were the real reason our main characters even ended up together.

Now that I hopefully smoothed any ruffled feathers, here is some *factual* information on male victims of domestic violence. I could never hope to do this topic justice and I certainly wouldn't try in the back matter of a novella, so I'll let the professionals do the talking for me.

If you're sensitive to discussions centering around domestic violence, this may be hard to read. I don't blame you for skipping it. You already got the gist of it in the story itself, but I know some people like facts, so here they are, straight from the experts.

Men Can Be Victims of Abuse Too[1]

At the Hotline, we know that domestic violence can affect anyone – including men. According to the CDC, one in seven men age 18+ in the U.S. has been the victim of severe physical violence by an intimate partner in his lifetime. One in 10 men has experienced rape, physical violence, and/or stalking by an intimate partner. In 2013, 13% of documented contacts to The Hotline identified themselves as male victims.

Although they make up a smaller percentage of callers to The Hotline, there are likely many more men who do not report or seek help for their abuse, for a variety of reasons:

- Men are socialized not to express their feelings or see themselves as victims.
- Pervading beliefs or stereotypes about men being abusers, women being victims.
- The abuse of men is often treated as less serious, or a "joke."
- Many believe there are no resources or support available for male victims.

No matter what your situation is, **The Hotline is here to help**, confidentially and without judgment. Please give us a call anytime, or chat online with us 24/7/365.

Myths Around Men Experiencing Abuse[2]

Talking about abuse and domestic violence can be a difficult task for anyone. It can be painful, confusing and make you feel ashamed, inadequate, and isolated. However, it can be incredibly challenging for men due to stereotypes, fear, misinformation, and societal pressures that men experience. These myths around men experiencing abuse can affect many different parts of their journey to a safer place.

We know that **domestic violence does not discriminate** when it comes to gender. But, men seem not to report abuse in the same way women do. In fact, many men remain silent because they think there's no point in reporting the abuse. They think no one will ever believe them.

Myths around men experiencing abuse (and why they're just myths):

Myth #1: The world tells us that men can't be victims of abuse.

> We know that **1 in 10 men** have experienced rape, physical violence and/or stalking by an intimate partner. And yet, we also hear from our male contacts that they are not believed or taken seriously when reporting the abuse to family members, friends, or law enforcement. On average, **24 people** per minute are victims of rape, physical violence, or stalking by an intimate partner. So violence *can* and *does* happen to men too!

Myth #2: The media tells us men are just the perpetrators of violence, but never the victims.

> **"Contribution of Media to the Normalization and Perpetuation of Domestic Violence"** shows that DV has become pervasive in society. It is partly

because of **media exposure** that we have **become desensitized** and even accustomed to it. According to this study, "chronic and repeated exposure to domestic violence is believed to cause changes in affective, cognitive, and behavioral processes." So, what happens when this repeated exposure only portrays men as perpetrators and not victims? *You get the idea.*

But make no mistake: domestic violence is not normal, and it's not a joke. It's not something we should readily accept as only happening to women. It happens to men too.

Myth #3: Men are not real men if they can't take it.

Male contacts tell us daily that they feel like less of a man when experiencing abuse in their relationships. Some have reported feeling so ashamed that they don't want to acknowledge the abuse. They fear that if they do, they will make the situation "real."

According to the **American Psychological Association**, stereotypes of masculinity can have a negative effect on young boys and men because they can stigmatize "normal human emotions." If a man feels stigmatized about what's happening to him, it's more likely he won't report the abuse. They might not want to talk about ways of dealing with it and their emotions. Feeling angry, scared, or sad is normal for all people experiencing abuse, regardless of sex, gender identity, or sexual orientation. Men don't have to "take it" (the abuse) to prove their masculinity.

Myth #4: Men don't have access to the same resources as women.

While there seem to be more **DV resources** for women than men, steps continue to be taken to change this. In Oct. 2017, the **Associated Press reported** that only the second shelter specifically for men was opening in Texas. Now, even more resources are available to men.

Myth #5: Men who are gay or bisexual will bring shame to the LGBTQ+ community if they report being victims of abuse.

It's already hard dealing with abuse when you are heterosexual, but gay or trans men experience even more challenges. Sometimes, we hear from some **LGBTQ+** contacts that reporting abuse in a same-sex or trans-relationship will bring "shame" to their community. They fear it will create more stereotypes or misinformation. Because of this, some people think this issue should only be dealt with behind closed doors. As Audre Lorde famously coined, "silence will not protect you." Regardless of what your sexual orientation is, it is always worth talking about abuse, and it's always worth **leaving.**

To combat these myths around men experiencing abuse, here are some ways to help men affected by abuse and domestic violence:

- Believe victims and survivors.
- Document the abuse.
- Find a support system.
- Take a proactive approach to your own safety.
- Reach out to The Hotline for help.

Further reading:

Kippert, Amanda. "A Guide for Male Survivors of Domestic Violence." Domestic Shelters. 13 Oct 2021. https://www.domesticshelters.org/articles/ending-domestic-violence/a-guide-for-male-survivors-of-domestic-violence

A series of articles and publications at https://mankind.org.uk/statistics/research-male-victims-of-domestic-abuse/

Various statistics on male survivors of domestic violence in the UK at https://mankind.org.uk/statistics/statistics-on-male-victims-of-domestic-abuse/

---

1. "Men Can Be Victims of Abuse Too." National Domestic Violence Hotline. n.d. https://www.thehotline.org/resources/men-can-be-victims-of-abuse-too/
2. "Myths Around Men Experiencing Abuse." National Domestic Violence Hotline. n.d. https://www.thehotline.org/resources/myths-around-men-experiencing-abuse/

Resources

This is by no means a comprehensive list, but it *is* a starting point for those who—God forbid—may need it.

While the focus of the majority of these organizations is on ending domestic violence and abuse, a lot of them have a variety of information to assist men in other areas of their life, such as divorce, family court, drug addictions, etc.

United States

National Domestic Violence Hotline
CALL 800-799-SAFE(7233)
SMS Text START to 88788
CHAT live at https://www.thehotline.org/

The Network/La Red (LGBTQ-specific resources)
CALL 800-832-1901 or 617-742-4911
VISIT The Network/La Red's 24-hour hotline

Local resources available at https://www.thehotline.org/get-help/domestic-violence-local-resources/

To find a local shelter, go to https://www.domesticshelters.org/help#?page=1.

For more information and resources for male survivors of sexual abuse, visit https://malesurvivor.org/.

Canada

Canadian Centre for Men and Families
CALL 647-479-9611 or 844-900-CCMF(2263)
EMAIL info@menandfamilies.org
VISIT https://menandfamilies.org/

United Kingdom & Ireland

ManKind Initiative
CALL 01823 334244
VISIT https://mankind.org.uk/

Galop (LGBTQ-specific resources)
CALL 0800 999 5428
EMAIL help@galop.org.uk
CHAT at https://galop.org.uk/get-help/helplines/

Abused Men In Scotland (AMIS)
CALL 03300 949 395
EMAIL support@amis.org.uk
VISIT https://abusedmeninscotland.org/

Men's Aid Ireland
CALL 01 554 3811

EMAIL Hello@mensaid.ie
VISIT https://www.mensaid.ie/

Australia

One in Three Campaign offers a number of crisis hotlines.

Germany

National Helpline
CALL 49 800 123 99 00

Acknowledgments

I'll keep this one short and sweet, like this novella was supposed to be… before I went and Drewek-ed it up with some death and violence.

Nisha—thank you for loving this story from the very beginning, even when it wasn't the best, and for encouraging me to release it on its own. Thank you for *all* that you do. When Edgar gets out of control, I know I can count on you to put him back in the box.

Lori—thank you for reading this story, like, a hundred times and offering your input with each draft. You help make all of my stories stronger and I'm so grateful. And thank you for "the curse of Faye." It tied the whole thing together beautifully! I'm sorry she's not buried under the rose bushes. It would have been a *much* more satisfying ending, honestly. It's my one regret with this story.

My husband—even though he'll never read this, I have to give him a shout-out. Aside from everything he does in our day-to-day lives to make things better for our family, he was also a source of inspiration for the big/awful things that happened in the book in a roundabout way. The explosion at Zane's father's job? Happened at my husband's job. The severe car accident caused by an angry girlfriend yanking on the steering wheel? Happened to my husband's friend. Oh, and he also picked out the squiggly heart in the dedication (although it may not be visible, depending on how you're reading this book. But it's super cute, so I put it below, too).

Also by Ashlyn Drewek

The Leander Welles Series:

THE MYSTERY OF LEANDER WELLES — a dark, psychological romantic suspense about a criminal psychiatrist who falls in love with her patient. *Finalist for Suspense in the 2021 Next Generation Indie Book Awards.*

THE RATIONALE OF LEANDER WELLES — a dark, psychological romantic suspense about an alleged murderer who falls in love with his psychiatrist... or does he?

THE DAMNATION OF LEANDER WELLES: OR, THE DEATH & LIFE OF BENNETT REEVE — a dark MM friends-to-lovers romance about a cutthroat lawyer and an enigmatic millionaire and what happens when two dark souls join forces. *A prequel to Book 1 and 2.*

THE WRATH OF LEANDER WELLES — a dark, MM romantic suspense about love, revenge, and how far a psychopath is willing to go for both.

The Solnyshko Duet:

THE KIDNAPPING OF ROAN SINCLAIR — a dark MM romance about an American college guy who is kidnapped by a Russian criminal.

THE VENGEANCE OF ROAN SINCLAIR — a dark MM romance about love in the aftermath of trauma and finding your new normal.

The Tennebrose Series

CALIGO — a short MM story about an eager grad student, his "crazy" history professor, and a trip to the woods in search of the infamous Winslow Witch. This is a newsletter exclusive.

MALUM DISCORDIAE — a dark academia MM enemies-to-lovers paranormal romance about witches, Necromancers, and a blood feud that has lasted centuries.

IGNI FERROQUE — a dark MM paranormal romance about a pious Necromancer and an incorrigible demon and what happens when their paths intersect.

MORTEM OBIRE — a dark MM paranormal best-friends-to-lovers romance about secrets and ghosts. Coming October 2023.

Paranormal & Dark Fantasy Standalones:

THE COVENTRY CAROL — a darker MM Christmas novella with hot Santa smut, anti-Christmas feels, and a cannibal hitman.

PER SANGUINEM — a slow-burn paranormal MM romantic suspense standalone about vampires and cops with commitment issues and what happens when you fall in love with your partner.

Contemporary Standalones:

BRIAR & BRAMBLE — a darker Valentine's Day MM novella about ex-stepbrothers, old wounds, and second chances. This was originally published in the *Anti-Valentine* anthology and is now exclusive to my website and newsletter.

About the Author

International best-selling and award-winning dark romance author Ashlyn Drewek has always been a hopeless romantic. She's also fascinated by the dark, macabre things in life such as Halloween, murder, cemeteries, and witchcraft. Not necessarily in that order.

Most of her time is spent making up stories in her head or researching obscure historical topics. The results of those efforts usually end up in a book as some sort of weird Easter egg or symbolism. Anything to make Edgar Allan Poe proud.

For information on news, upcoming releases, and where to find Ashlyn on social media, check out the QR code below.

Made in United States
Troutdale, OR
01/12/2025

27875164R10083